happy,
technically.

a novella

happy,
technically.
a novella

MARC GEFFEN

PHILADELPHIA

FIRST DEPTH DEPARTMENT EDITION, NOVEMBER 2018

All rights reserved. Published by Depth
Department, Philadelphia, Pennsylvania.

DEPTH
DEPT.

ISBN-10: 0692175261
ISBN-13: 978-0692175262

www.depthdepartment.com

Cover design by Becki Kozel

for Foster

PART ONE

1

I broke the seal of the envelope, barely avoiding a paper cut. The instant ecstasy of relief washed over me as I looked down at a wrinkle underneath one of my knuckles, skin still completely intact. That could have been a fucking disaster.

My parents had sent me a card, one that I'm sure was chosen with great care from a stationery section in one of those pharmacy convenience stores. Drugs, candies, and outsourced salutations, all waiting on shelves to make us feel good, conveniently. I imagined my father standing in an aisle, my mother consulting through the phone at his ear as he scanned an array of categorized cards — "BIRTHDAY," "THANK YOU," "BLANK" — trying to find a fold of paper injected with the appropriate degree of sentiment yet unable to concentrate amid the incomprehensible mess: mismatched envelopes, celebratory cards in the "SYMPATHY" section, anarchy.

A cartoon bear pranced on the front of the card in

a cap and gown, a diploma in his paw. The image made me think about how I'd been hibernating for the past four years: sleeping for most of each day, droning on, referring to a circuit of scheduled events as life's to-do list. I should have emerged fit and hungry, fat trimmed and mind eager. Instead, I greeted the springtime with several extra pounds and all ambition weighed down by beer. And fear.

I flipped open the card. "Welcome to the real world!" said the bear's wise parents, pictured inside. "Live your dreams, honey!" I had just graduated from a reputable university and also from a previous self. Schooling was over. Next year no longer came with an outline or clear expectations, no apparent grade classification. *You're a derailed train*, I thought to myself.

vividandvague.com/blog/entry=1

I am Andersen.

At this point, I am twenty-two years into
a life that's starting to gradually blur, or
perhaps come into focus; it's hard to tell. I
began archiving ideas through writing because,
unfortunately, my brain doesn't have a printer,
and I myself have a hard time interpreting its
messages without externalizing them. So this is
the only way to spew the collage of thoughts
that I've been collecting onto someone else,
into open space, before taking it all off-line,
if you will. I've reached that moment when the
brain begins to drift away and, whispering back
to itself through an unsuspecting ear, implores:
"Shut the fuck up."

Andersen is actually my middle name. I'm
using it here because it feels like a better
representation of the version of myself that I
want to be. My first name is for the character
that I project out in the real world, away from
this spill-my-mind-on-the-internet experiment.

happy, technically.

My last name is a sign of my pedigree, my coat of arms, a nod to where I'm from. *Where I am*, on the other hand, is my middle name — in limbo between the character and the artifact, comfortable as the arbitrary self, the thing that is simply because it is not other things.

A bit more about me, for the record and for the love of context: I have a small family, and I like it that way. It makes it easier to view myself as an independent being, with few ties to the past and less influence from layers of familial relationships compared to most. Maybe I'm less programmed and possess more novel sentiment to offer my small circle, the few I do call family, the few I love. Whether I share it frequently enough is a different story. I've been a bit reclusive and quite self-aware lately — on a mission to find out what my self is and destroy it, probably.

Within the last year, I've become eerily conscious of my consciousness, and the past has come into focus: years and layers of untruth fortified by time and ubiquity, my perspective drenched in the wake of previous thinkers like a dirtied lens. I have uncovered foreignness at a hyper-local level but confirmed no intruder; this, one in a series of incisive syllogisms, has catalyzed the end of a certain era of *me*. Up to this point, events unraveled sequentially, only connected by chronology, the need for one occurrence to precede and influence the next.

happy, technically.

Now I'm picking up on clues in the minutiae that are beginning to reveal the blueprint for some larger, universal order of things.

Shit is about to hit the fan, but I can take solace in the fact that at least I'll no longer be full of shit.

2

When Nina's key turned the lock, I was standing in the kitchen with a towel around my waist, still wet from a shower, pouring myself a glass of whiskey. Three ice cubes crackled as booze hit the glass, and the familiarity of the sound signaled my brain to calm itself. I had decided that tonight would be the night I'd tell her what I had to tell her.

I returned the ice tray and, as I occasionally do, took a moment to look through the collage of memories and reminders on the refrigerator door, pressed beneath a scatter of magnets. The graduation card from my parents hung there, added almost three years earlier. I raised my glass to the educated bear.

Nina locked the door behind her with two clicks and sighed away a day's worth of stress. She caught my eyes and smiled curtly, perhaps recognizing the tension in my face. Her senses were in tune with mine, and we knew each other very well by this point, separate selves learning to be one. I was nervous but tried to hide it. I wanted to break the news in a way that felt dramatic, climactic. I was convinced that if she perceived profundity in the situation, I could make it so, manifesting a turning point in my time-line. The details — the towel around my waist, the whiskey — were my way of setting a scene, providing atmosphere for events to float in. Maybe it was just a play for control, but I'd been training as an actor for most of my life, so why not exercise my creative freedom here — you know, actually make some choices?

To clarify, I was an actor in the way we all are actors: fulfilling roles, working to project an affable personality, feigning normalcy for the convenience it pro-vides. Think of life's day-to-day auditions, the scripts of each interaction and relationship, the fake backdrop of what we'd otherwise all agree is "real." My profession, if you want to call it that, was digital advertising. I played a strategic planner, a role that supposedly entails research into human behavior, guiding the creative process with insights about people, to represent the voice of the con-sumer in ads made for the internet. If any consumer voice made it into the work we sold our clients, it was strained and hoarse, or resigned to a whimper.

I was unfulfilled. The week I graduated college, I signed on to join an ad agency. I'd been plotting my escape ever since.

o o o

"How was your day, babe?" I asked.

Nina shrugged and managed another half-smile before answering. "Long."

We were synced to the routine of long work days, wondering what the hell happened to the five in nine-to-five. It was now a quarter to nine, and we were just regaining our true personalities, disengaging autopilot. Friday nights often started like this, bound by the buzz of whiskey and a sense of newfound freedom. I'd get home first, hastily dispose of my office persona like a hit man dumping a dead body, then wash away the evidence with a shower before greeting Nina. If we were going out, she only had time for a costume change, so her workday intensity and dreams from the night before lingered, adding an extra dimension to her presence like a subtle perfume.

Nina took off her jacket and hung it on the coat rack. "Will you be ready soon?" she asked, on her way to the bedroom. "I'm gonna go get changed real quick, then let's go to Tway's party."

I sipped my whiskey, already a step ahead. Drops of water fell from my wet hair, collecting at my feet, ticking off the seconds before I'd have to tell her the news. For now, I stood in a shallow puddle of my own fear.

It was the start of our second year living together on 8th Street. The apartment was a one-bedroom railroad unit, a series of stacked rooms laid along parallel tracks. Our upstart, young-professional means left us without the luxury of hallways. The place resembled a sitcom set: One smooth dolly shot could capture a perfect cross-section of the entire apartment, a day in the life of Andersen and Nina. This layout gave our home a chronological feel, a sense that time spent living there flowed linearly, from one room to the next, each room designed to frame a scene — like this one, in which water beads onto the kitchen floor, evidence of my procrastination.

I need to tell her.

I quickly assembled an outfit, dressed, then went to sit in the living room while Nina rummaged through the bedroom closet, operating somewhere beyond my present state — the future, or possibly the past, depending on what room in the apartment you considered the beginning. Outside, this linear model of time crumbled, but chaos could not permeate the walls of our 8th Street home. Or so it felt.

"Hey, babe?" Nina called, peeking her head out of the bedroom.

I shifted some ice around in my mouth before answering. "Yeah?"

"Quick question. Do you like these shoes with the suede, or these, with the higher heel? I just got them today."

Despite her impeccable fashion sense, Nina always asked for my opinion of her outfits. And I always devoted a moment of genuine concentration before answering, though I knew that any advice I offered ultimately carried little weight. Her taste needed no reassurance.

She now stood before me, draped in a simple but expensive-looking dress, balancing between two different types of heel, turning slowly, offering different angles of her silhouette. Nina had a knack for shifting my perception with ease. I smiled, brought the glass to my lips and let another sip of whiskey burn a trail to my stomach. Everything felt warm for a moment. This was exactly who I wanted to be and where I wanted to be: a young man in his first home, legs outstretched on the coffee table, admiring a woman. The simplicity of my happiness stretched my smile. *I can tell her anything.*

After a pause, I let out what I knew she wanted to hear. "The higher heel, definitely." I'm a calculated guy, religious only in terms of my faith in logic. It was simple: 1) The higher heels were presented as the second option — people usually save the best for last, especially Nina; 2) it didn't really matter that there were two options. Clearly, the woman wants to wear her new shoes.

She approved and started to switch into the matching heel. That's when I let it out. I said it definitively, as if the words were a line in the sand. Nina kept her head lowered, perhaps taking a second to worry about our future, but it didn't freeze her; she continued to fiddle with the clasp of her shoe. After a moment, she looked up to check my expression, then took a swig of my whiskey. I watched her in what seemed like slow motion. Nina occupied precious real estate at the intersection of sexiness and elegance. She was the kind of brunette that made certain guys prefer brunettes.

"It was a matter of time, wasn't it?" she asked calmly.

"It's all a matter of time," I said. "This was a matter of timing."

It's 7:30 p.m. on a Tuesday night, and I'm sitting in a twenty-four-hour laundromat in Brooklyn. I wish it were 4 a.m. I want to be alone.

There's this guy here sitting across from me, breathing as if to keep tempo with his pacemaker. Replacing the air in his lungs is a conscious task, deliberate and metronomic. His breath, which I'm getting faint whiffs of, hints at his age — stale and ancient, like a relic from the 1930s, like he was pulled from the dusty attic of my younger generation. Thankfully, the tumbling dryers provide a calming white noise that creates distance between the two of us. I'm not comfortable with him loitering in my thought-space. There's only room for one here. And yet, truthfully, my discomfort stems from the fact that one day I may become him — a guy waiting for clothes to dry and cycles to end, investing energy in every taste of oxygen.

At some point, you begin to question if

any of it really matters, all that extrane-
ous shit we feel we must allow to fester in
our brain from day to day if we are to lead a
normal life. I'm talking about the thoughts that
bubble up in that anxious area of the brain,
the sliver of layered gray matter that somehow
fought all the other lobes in a battle of impor-
tance and emerged the victor. When the fuck did
this happen?

Anyway, I think I'm ready to do it, by the
end of this week. It has to be. I'm going to be
completely honest with the person I love about
my new views on life. I'm going to tell her that
I don't know exactly who I am, that I'm going to
quit my job to try and figure things out, that I
may not be able to provide the type of security
she needs or is expecting. I'm just going . . .

3

Nina had a few questions, but all in all, she reacted with an open mind and more understanding than I ever could have imagined. She listened and told me she loved me. I was drunk with gratitude.

We left the apartment and arrived at Tway's fashionably late and sufficiently buzzed. Situated on a vibrant corner in a hip neighborhood in the greatest city in the world, Tway's loft was one of those places that felt like a landmark for a very specific era. The apartment was our hive of creativity and blissful mania, but now it is in grave danger of becoming yesterday's scene as the culture spreads virulently eastward, relentless in search of nascent, fertile breeding ground. Welcome to the new New York.

I had lived in the city for seven years, dwelling in vertical space, making moments in the skyline. Life in New York tends to be very compartmentalized, unfurling in scenes between elevator rides. I spent less time in those Manhattan lifts now, though I often thought about how frequently I undulated between lows and highs. One button — a simple trigger — could send me up or down. And so I walked into Tway's operating under a worldview in flux.

Within twenty minutes at the party, I was down to a three-pack, caught in cordial but forced conversation. Introductions were flying left and right, friends of friends practicing politeness. Tway mentioned a road trip that he and I were planning (with no direction or conviction) and asked others for ideas. Then, a misstep in the niceties: Someone asked me about *what I do*, and I guess I threw a few people by answering with an offbeat response about *who I am*. There was nervous laughter. Nina shot a sympathetic glance my way, but she must have thought I was beginning to lose it. Things trended toward awkwardness, and I excused myself.

Walking away from the chatter, I cracked another beer and reveled in that awkwardness. Somehow my detachment felt fashionable. Then, I immediately thought about what an asshole I was. *You're going to talk about who you are, as if you're sure of it? You think all this ad-libbing is clever?* It's natural to open up from time to time, to fully let your guard down, as you do when strolling around the house in nothing but underwear, unashamed and unconcerned with who's around. But one time your dick slips through the slot for an inappropriate audience, and it's then you quickly realize that people tolerate different degrees of openness, accept truth at different frequencies.

Still wandering the party, I found the bar, an oasis in a desert of dry small talk. The selection was meager by that point, but the scavengers had left a little bourbon, the bite my beer couldn't provide. I scanned for other supplies and thought about swigging straight from the bottle. Just needed a taste to swallow my internal arguments.

"Cups and ice are in the cooler below," someone said. I turned to see a guy, tall-ish and slender but visibly fit, probably a runner, standing by Tway's bookshelf, pointing to the bar. His short, dark hair and similarly dark monochromatic outfit accented his very blue, glacial eyes. "You mind making me one?" he asked.

I nodded. Sure, why not share the recipe? I poured out two on the rocks and joined him.

"Thanks for the drink. Check this out," he said, waving me toward the bookshelf, forgoing introductions. He was quick with words but full of focus. "It's amazing what you can learn about people without directly asking anything. If you feel the spine of a book, you can tell whether or not it's been read. There's a fine ridge that surfaces when the pages have been turned, loosening the binding."

He turned to the shelf and skimmed his fingers over a row of books, reading the collection like it was braille. I watched, amused, confused, and content to not talk.

"It seems Tway isn't really a fan of fiction," he said.

Before committing to a full-fledged conversation, I looked to see if Nina was nearby in case I needed an out. She wasn't far, though she didn't seem to be holding me in her periphery; she was fixed in conversation with a couple I'd never seen before — completely un-awkwardly, of course.

"I'm Andersen," I said, shaking hands.

"Sevi. Nice to meet you. You a friend of Tway's?"

I gave him the backstory in CliffsNotes: Tway and I grew up together in a suburb of Philadelphia, went off to different New York colleges, then ended up living a few blocks apart in Brooklyn after graduation. I asked how they knew each other.

"He's one of my beta-testers. Applied through a Facebook ad and showed up at the office about two weeks ago. I run a tech startup, and we've got a few freelancers helping us test our first product."

"Sounds like Tway," I said, half-laughing. "He's made a career for himself doing odd jobs." I remembered visiting Tway on his lunch hour at the dealership where he washed cars (and sold weed) during high school summers. Throughout sophomore year of college, he practically had a residency at a sperm bank in Queens. Now he was floating in the startup economy. "So, what are you making . . . this, uh, first product?" I asked.

"Well, it's quite complicated," Sevi said, without a touch of pretentiousness. "If you're into the technical side of things . . ."

I nodded. "Yeah, actually. I work — I mean, I used to work — in digital strategy, so I'm familiar with the space. Plus, if Tway's involved, it must be interesting."

He accepted the invite. "Ultimately, we want to leverage data for reasons that are far more ambitious than traditional marketing uses, like improved targeting, efficient pricing, and whatnot. That's all been done twice over. Our aim is to use personal data and machine learning to help people find their true happiness — to show them patterns in their behavior and make recommendations for life decisions based on that information. I started the company about eighteen months ago, and we've secured a first round of funding, so now we're working hard to get our beta version in market."

I blinked a few times, trying to refresh the image in my head of a venture capitalist signing over multiple millions based on that pitch.

Sevi sensed my skepticism. "I told you it's complicated. It can be difficult to grasp without seeing our applications in action. Basically, we start collecting an array of data once a user opts in to the platform. All digital actions — site visits, social media interactions, e-commerce purchases — they become data points. We call it a stream. It's the story of who we all are, our preferences and tendencies. For example," he continued, "I now know a lot about what Tway has and hasn't read, and so I can make strong inferences about his interests or recent frame of mind."

We both examined the bookshelf and took a swig from our drinks. "You didn't even have to come to his home for that. Just access his Amazon profile, right?" I said.

"Right, or, at least, we can use that as a very good proxy. We can feed that type of information to our system, run it against other data points from his stream, and start to understand how exposure to certain content and experiences — like the novels he's read and the trips he's taken — likely influence his behavior. Where it really gets interesting," he said, genuinely enthralled by his explanation, "is taking the next step to emotion: periodically asking the user about how they feel. What makes them happy, what's troubling them. What are their goals? That's where our technology transcends value as a marketing tool or recommendation engine or whatever. We're tapping into streams of data to uncover knowledge to optimize the lives we lead. It's psychoanalysis on a scale never attempted."

I was intrigued, but the empty Solo cup and my dwindling six-pack brought my attention to my bladder, which begged for relief. I told Sevi I'd be right back but wanted to hear more.

"Listen," he said, "I'm gonna get out of here. Getting pretty late. Really nice to meet you, man." We shook again. "You should stop by the office some time. I can show you what we're working on, and maybe we can grab a drink with Tway."

"What's the best way to get in touch?" I asked.

"We're called Enlightenment Labs," he said. His

eyes shot across the apartment and fixed on the front door. "Google it."

I briefly traced Sevi's movement through the crowded party as he walked away. Remembering I had to take a leak, I then weaved my own route through the party toward the bathroom.

Enjoying a possible world-record piss, I wondered: Could it work? Did Sevi's startup uniquely fill a void in the market? Isn't everyone looking for profit in happiness? The onset of my drunkenness drowned out the coherence of any thought I could muster around these questions. Washing my hands, my ruminating mood remained. I caught my own eyes in the mirror and held on long enough for their depths to reveal a sick joke: I may never reach the bottom, may never understand what is behind my eyes interpreting the images they perceive.

I walked back into the party. It was just after 1 a.m., and most of the unfamiliar faces had disappeared, fading out of focus. I did a quick search and found Nina; she was welcoming Jenn, one of her friends from work who had just showed up. On my way over to them, I was intercepted by Jeff and Leo, our good friends. They had their hands full, trying to balance a bunch of shots.

"Whatup, man?" Leo said, handing me a drink. "The last of the tequila. Not the good stuff, but fuck it!"

We joined the girls, toasted, and picked up from where we all left off the last time we were together, maybe two weeks before, maybe a month — the gap was inconsequential.

The shots went down smoothly and the conversation warmed me, but my energy waned. I couldn't bring myself to join everyone; they'd started dancing, and I felt too cerebral. So I sunk into the couch, further rewinding my conversation with Sevi. I wondered if my stream would interest him. Am I leaving behind valuable data, dropping breadcrumbs worth following? In some strange way, the encounter separated me from the others. Lost in a song, content with the couch and my thoughts, I watched my friends vibe out from a distance.

Tonight, there was a party after a party, and only those who actually matter were there, survivors of the debauchery. The late-night crew is always family, and the late-night energy is healthy, an intangible but invigorating aura, an agent of expression. A great song was playing, draping the scene in tones that fit the mood like a glove, releasing audible dyes that painted the room perfectly.

I saw the connectivity, the linkages that create a network of friends, each a reflection of and an influence on a great companionship. The ostensible intricacy of our relationships dissolved, revealing simple truths as to why we share so many experiences in this life, why some fateful spider caught us all in the same web. Tonight, beats and booze were the spider's silk, entangling my friends in a moment and giving us the gift of time.

4

Saturday morning. Our bodies floated haphazardly within the waves of a faded yellow duvet cover, a comfortable mess of deadweight. Slivers of sunlight battled the window curtain and teased our eyelids, begging for a chance to warm our pupils. It was the least the sun could do; after all, I dedicated several minutes each day to admiring its form and to wondering how the hell it got there.

Nina woke as I rustled our linen bedding. Leaning over for a good-morning kiss, she winced at the taste of alcohol on my breath. I'm not a big drinker, but from time to time I do enjoy inebriation as a lens through which to see the world. I opted for that perspective the night before and was paying for it this morning.

Unfortunately, sleeping it off wasn't really an option. Up early is a routine. I can't sleep past 8 a.m. on any given day and used to think my internal clock was perpetually synced to the schedule of the work week. Then I realized that I subconsciously rouse myself from sleep because my mind is paranoid about not wasting the limited time of its life. So I tend to rise in this way, agitated yet geared for productivity.

After rolling out of bed, I walked mechanically to the window, one hand covering a yawn, the other buried in my boxers — standard morning adjustments. I pulled the curtain aside and looked back at Nina, the sleepyhead. She caught my stare through the sunlight and focused her squint, first in my direction and then over to the clock. The 7:47 a.m. readout made her sigh and fall back into the pillow heap.

"Ugh," she groaned. "I feel shitty. Are you hungover?"

"Nope," I said, through a facetious smile. "Just hung."

With a sputter of energy, she performed a theatrical eye roll, and then, almost instantly, fell back asleep.

o o o

I chugged two glasses of water in the kitchen before crawling back into bed to read for a little while. Once Nina woke for good, we spent the morning lying there, staring up at the off-white ceiling, a blank slate for our ideas. We talked for nearly two hours, though I did more of the listening at first. Nina gathered her personal secrets and let them leak, spilling onto and into me.

"I've been thinking about what you told me last

night. I think I dreamed about it, actually," she said. "It didn't surprise me that much — I could tell you haven't been happy at work. And I support you moving on, I really do." She paused, running a hand through her hair a few times. "But, to be honest, it makes me kind of nervous."

I reached out to hold her hand. "Of course," I said. "Me too. I'm more than nervous. I'm scared. But I'm sure, babe. I don't know my next move, and that's definitely what's scary, but there's something urging me to get moving, a thing I've never really felt before."

Our eyes met, confirming an unspoken understanding: We both knew I was talking about more than just a job. But we continued to use that construct to talk about the bigger things.

"You're good at what you do, Andersen. And I always saw you getting better and rising up the ranks, and that being a big part of us building a life together. I don't want you to give up so much of what you've worked for just because, I don't know . . . just because you're restless."

That one hit home, but I didn't have the energy for defensiveness. I was, actually, a little hungover.

"It's more than restlessness, though," I said. "It's like I've already moved on, but I wake up every day and give everything I've got for a reason I *used* to care about, for people I *used* to admire. I'm over it." It felt good to be honest about my decision, and I knew Nina would at least hear me out.

I kept it coming. "Advertising is absurd. A bunch

of people convinced they're, like, shepherding the culture in some creative, better direction. But we're just fucking marionettes, and the strings are money, not creativity. I'm leaving the business."

"I get it, but isn't that —"

"The job is one thing," I cut her off. The confession was flowing. "I could probably stick with it for a while longer. What I can't tolerate, though, is being scared of being scared. I'm terrified to leave just because it will put me in an uncomfortable place, if only for a short while. There's something pathetic about that, right? I need to know that I won't give in to that."

Nina sensed my conviction, I think, and didn't try to persuade me otherwise. Something in her body language suggested relief. A sigh made without a sound. Maybe we were actually talking to one another about different things. I second-guessed my intuition about what she was thinking. But when you second-guess, you realize you were just guessing, even at first.

"What was your dream?" I asked.

"What?"

"You said you had a dream last night," I said.

"Oh." Nina took a few deep, expressive breaths, then sat up. "I don't remember exactly," she said. "It was very real though. Not a nightmare at all, but one of those dreams that's eerie because it feels so normal, you know? And when you play it back, the normalcy feels too close to home to be happening when you're not conscious. Anyway, it was sort of a collage of us in different situations, nothing out of the ordinary, except something between us was —" She hesitated, looked around for a second, then grabbed a pillow to fill her lap. She fixed her eyes there. "Something was just *off*. You were kind of, uh, more unsure about everything. Unsure about us."

I started to say something, but this time it was her turn to interrupt.

"Look, I get it," she continued, anticipating my words. "This isn't just about you quitting, though. This also isn't just about you, in general. I'm realizing it's about me too. I can't stop thinking about the future, even in my sleep, apparently. It's gotten to the point where all I do is speculate. I'm obsessed with what's next because I want to get my guard up before it happens, I think. It's like my version of being scared of being scared."

The light, which had been splintered and sharp, found a comfortable angle through the window and settled into the room more fully.

"Think of it this way," I said. "The near future is an imminent past, and your distant future is death. Neither of those deserve your attention."

Nina sort of twitched and slowly craned her head to look me in the eye. "That's fucking depressing, babe," she said, rising from the bed. "Let's get some food. I'm starving."

I'm not the kind of guy who procrastinates. Like, when I buy a loaf of bread, I'll use the two shitty end pieces for my first sandwich. Last week, I had a revelation that I was deeply unhappy at my job. This week, I gave my two weeks' notice. Not without a hitch, though.

Just before meeting with my boss, I found myself marooned in a bathroom stall for what was, let's just say, an unpleasant amount of time. It happens. Strong coffee. Or maybe nerves. Sitting there, I had a moment to take inventory of some curious thoughts while rehearsing the "I quit" spiel in my head, thoughts about what it means to sit with yourself, to be deep in thought and consider your own multitudes. I took out my phone to save a few notes:

Our conscience, that familiar self/voice/ soul/conductor orchestrating everything, needs to be alone sometimes. So we grant it solitude and let it devise a way to teach us. For a moment. And that is really a beautiful moment of self-recognition and discovery of duality: There are two of you, and only one can survive. There exists an awkward relationship between these two selves, and the confusing tension therein is the catalyst for understanding, the key to evolution.

I slid the phone back into my pocket and continued to think about this idea of merging two selves into one, and how a new career might make that integration possible, before being cruelly brought back down to earth and realizing the predicament I was in.

There was no more toilet paper. There was nothing that resembled toilet paper, nothing paper-like, no tissue, no napkin, no soft alternative. *Are you fucking kidding me?* I looked down and acknowledged my last resort, comprehended the reality of the situation, and made peace with my pathetic immediate future. Despite all my good work — the big work, all of the intellectual toiling and the noble existentialism — here I was, wiping my ass with a sock. The universe looked on with a mischievous grin as one profound moment of thought morphed into an epic snafu, absurdity making an appearance to try and derail progress.

I did what I had to do and moved on, walking into my boss's office with one ankle completely bare. Then I sat across from her and

happy, technically.

did the other thing I had to do: I quit.

5

About a week into unemployment, the sheen wore off of my newfound freedom from the daily grind. I was actually handling the withdrawal pretty well, resisting the urge to crawl back to the security of an office. What I couldn't shake, though, was this nagging feeling that a fulfilling career may still be out there waiting for me. A job with nutritional value. I ended up doing what I had, in fact, decided to do a few weeks earlier while observing the late-night party from Tway's couch, slightly drunk, medium-rare high, and half-meditating on my future: I looked up Enlightenment Labs.

A quick Google search led me to the office number. I called, which seemed to catch the person who answered off guard. She was surprised not by the fact that *I* called but by the fact that someone *actually called*, and she was now in the unfamiliar position of conducting business over the phone. I explained that I'd recently met Sevi at an event and wanted to reconnect. The woman kindly assured me that she'd relay the message to him and asked for my email.

By that evening, I had a response direct from Sevi. A short, unvarnished email:

> Glad you got in touch. I figured you might.
> Assuming you're free, let's meet Thursday at 9:30.
> Just check in with Lex when you get here (she's
> the one you phoned).
> -Sevi

He *figured*? I focused on this word. Did our conversation at the bookshelf leave some kind of impression on him as well? I assumed those types of encounters were commonplace for him, a subtle yet strange way to pitch his startup. When he suddenly left the party mid-conversation, my own "figuring" suggested he was simply bored. But maybe he gleaned something from me and was satisfied to walk away, or perhaps he intended the abrupt exit to catch my attention. Who knows? Either way, at least I now had something on the docket for the week. I replied to confirm that I'd be there, then closed the computer and went to wash up for the night.

I do my best thinking in the shower. Under the water, thoughts rain down, and I am in the moment and I am cleansed. Then I do my best forgetting as I towel off. It's a shame. Something about standing there naked and catching a glimpse of myself in the mirror humanizes the ideas too much. A frame holding skin, drying, I am all too conscious of my need to remove the dirt I've collected, a day's worth of fallibility.

Sometimes I get lucky later in my routine, recalling fragments as I brush my teeth or towel-dry my hair. Here is one that I lost momentarily but recaptured while flossing, unable to shake my thoughts of Sevi and the oddity of our meeting: *Personality is an aesthetic*, not so much a natural incandescence of identity as it is the design of an essence, a way of emitting the heat of living through the controlled glow of a particular hue.

I took that to bed and the thought remained when I awoke. For the next two days, with no career to define my schedule or my purpose, I moseyed around the neighborhood coffee shops, bookstores, and bars thinking about the next personality I would design for myself.

o o o

Thursday started with the first alarm I had set all week. Nina and I shared the bathroom as we got ready for our respective days. She was chatty, seemingly cheered by the fact that I had something productive to do beyond lie in our bed for hours and bum around the apartment. I asked about her day ahead.

"It's gonna be super busy," she said, then mentioned something about multiple clients visiting the studio in Brooklyn. It was a bit hard to understand her.

Toothpaste frothed at the corners of her mouth as we tried to talk and brush our teeth at the same time, huddling close around our small sink. We had this running joke that tiny bathrooms forged healthy relationships and we should be thankful for our cramped quarters; naturally, couples must grow apart when they graduate to a "his and hers" vanity. Funny what you tell yourself to make your situation more comfortable.

Our morning routines soon diverged. I stood in front of the bedroom mirror, pulling on a shirt, when I heard her yell from the bathroom, "Can we take the train together? Or are you heading into Manhattan?"

"Nah," I shouted, "Manhattan."

We'd be taking different trains, as usual. Enlightenment Labs was in Tribeca; coincidentally, it was not far from my previous office, about six or seven blocks north. That change meant an additional ten-minute-or-so walk from the subway. Better leave ASAP.

I scanned the apartment for my bag, trying to find the articles of my once put-together commuter self. Eventually, decently dressed and computer bag in hand, I started for the door.

Nina intercepted me. "Good luck," she said.

"It's not an interview, you know."

That amused her. She smiled and kissed my fore-head. An endearing, motherly peck that suggested she knew something I didn't. "I know. But I can tell you're excited about it." Her hands moved upward toward my face, to pull me in for a real kiss, I thought. But she fingered my collar instead, unfolding a crumpled bit of material so it lay flat. "I love you," she said.

"Ditto, kiddo," I said, reaching for the door knob. Some routines are harder to shake.

The commute was instinctual: I moved with the sun, rising in the east and heading westward via the subway. At the end of the line, I exited, climbed the ramp at 14th Street and 8th Avenue and meandered toward the downtown A train. During this transfer, the people of New York engulfed me. The crowd like a school of fish — dead fish, really — capitulating to the urban current. I became one of them, and we collectively passed by the dead paper-people handing out two varieties of dead trees, *Metro* and *AM New York*. *Who reads this shit?* I wondered.

I also wondered about Sevi. From one quick meeting, I concocted an almost mythical image of him in my mind. But why? I replayed our original conversation as the train car twisted through the underground. He seemed like a big deal — certainly different from all these other commuter people, the rise-and-grind public, the sheep. He's a guy who seemed to have it all figured out.

o o o

Sure enough, a woman named Lex stood behind a mounted iPad at the entrance of the office. I checked in and told her that I had a 9:30 with Sevi.

39

"Welcome. I'll let him know you're here" she said. Her fingers deftly swiped and tapped the tablet with little assistance from her eyes, which, for the most part, still met mine. "While you wait, would you like any coffee or something?"

I heard her but other thoughts distracted my reply as I took in the sights and sounds of the office behind her. The place was both sterile and abuzz at the same time. It actually did look like a lab, one that operated in celebration of itself. The atmosphere of the entrepreneur. *This is exciting*, I thought, as if answering Nina.

Lex's voice broke in again. "We've got espresso and cold-pressed juice."

I responded quickly this time: "Yes." This non-choice made sense to her, apparently. She left her post at the iPad and walked over to a nearby island, a café station of sorts, transitioning from receptionist to barista. Startup fluidity.

I watched her grab a bottled juice from a small fridge, then go to work at a La Marzocco, tapping and pulling. Colorfully dressed employees shuffled around her, vibrant pops of life against the gallery-white floors, walls, and ceilings. Some sat together at small café tables, hunched over open laptops or phones, or devices that dissolved any distinction between the two. The whole space looked like an open-concept kitchen designed for a dorm at MIT.

"Here you go," Lex said a few moments later,

handing me both drinks. "Feel free to grab a seat; he should be with you in a sec."

"Thanks very much," I said.

I turned to scan the room for an open chair but got distracted by various movements in the teeming lobby. A guy video-chatting in full stride, arm extended as a mount for his device; Lex greeting a new visitor at her iPad; the espresso machine starting up again. I looked on as two women began to write on one section of the whiteboard wall. They alternated between blue and red marker, imposing colorful code on the otherwise pristine blank space, new ideas overtaking purity.

When Sevi showed up shortly thereafter, extending his hand for a shake, I was caught standing idly among the lab activity, double-fisting. I quickly threw back the espresso like a shot of tequila and grasped his hand.

"Great to see you," he said. "Welcome to Enlightenment."

With Sevi leading, we began to walk and talk. He showed me through the office, guiding with literal and figurative steps forward. I learned a lot in twenty-five minutes. The tour was surprisingly impassioned, a manifesto delivered in stride, and my previous impressions of Sevi — suggestive fragments from our initial encounter — solidified into a complete image. This guy was not your average entrepreneur. Not your average person at all, really. Philosophical tones gave wings to each of his words, flying ideas to loftier heights, to intellectual and spiritual places beyond the altitude of my comprehension.

Sevi projected with the confidence of a man who knows certain venerated secrets and enunciated as if to prove the sharpness of his mind. At one point, as we passed a string of small rooms furnished in the style of recording studios, he described how qualitative user interviews factor into Enlightenment's process. "Immersive interviews are a key part of our work stream. We invite consumers — you know, average folks — to come in for a couple hours and talk one-on-one with people from our Insights team. Depending on briefs from the product managers and engineers, these may be structured discussions designed to shed light on a certain product problem, but more often than not they unravel as organic conversation. Almost like a free therapy session." He paused, retracing mental steps. "Well, actually, we do compensate the participants. Great deal, right?"

"In my previous role, my team mostly relied on quantitative methods, but I had started to lean more toward user research in the last six months or so," I said.

He acknowledged this with an obliging nod before continuing. "Win-win. It really separates us from other machine-learning businesses. These in-depth interviews illuminate truths that inform our programming. We believe the architecture of future human experiences should reflect not only day-in-the-life data but also the deep, most instinctual urges of the psyche."

The tour ended as Sevi slid open a frosted glass

door, and we entered his office. Floor-to-ceiling windows framed a shot of the Freedom Tower — a beautiful view. It felt like glimpsing the future, looking out and knowing the same view used to reveal a different landscape, used to hold very different meaning. Maybe it was just the wheatgrass-espresso mix coursing through my veins, but I felt a head rush come on. A mix of inspiration and exhaustion. I was glad to grab a seat.

Sevi swung around the desk and dropped into his seat too, though he didn't let up on the intensity. "When I heard you were coming in, I looked into you, you know," he said. Sevi wasn't socially awkward, exactly — he just never downshifted to pleasantries, instead sustaining the self-possessed posture of an autodidact. "Chat" probably didn't play much of a role in his vocabulary.

I didn't reply to his admission of the background check. Waiting for him to show more of his hand, I felt my eyes narrow to a squint, more a mien of confusion than a defensive retort. Maybe Nina was right; I regretted shrugging off her offer of luck.

"Nothing too intense," he said, continuing in a reassuring tone, a disarmament. "I just talked to Tway, checked out your LinkedIn, read some of the blogs you've published. I realized I talked a lot about myself when we met at the party. Didn't get to hear much about you."

"So, find anything good?" I asked.

"Seems like you're developing into a pretty good researcher," he said, cutting to the chase.

"Well," I hesitated, surprised by the compliment. "Thank you. But 'pretty' insinuates some sort of lack." The awkward beat of silence that followed confirmed we were not yet familiar with each other's senses of humor. Sevi then conceded a smile. Flashes of confidence seemed to win him over. In turn, I accepted that he was snooping out of habitual diligence, not skepticism.

From there, we settled into conversation on an even playing field, discussing his grand vision for Enlightenment Labs and the company's intent to digitize psychotherapy. This was to be the ultimate social contribution of his life, he explained: to help individuals better understand their behavior and their state of mind, to better cope, to thrive in a world of increasing complexity. Talking about these topics, I found myself recalibrated to Sevi's wavelength of vehemence and headiness.

In this way, his intensity calmed me. It was a confirmation that everything really does matter, that the weightiness we feel is real and should be acknowledged and explored, and also that the way in which we deal with that weightiness is ripe for disruption. The examination of consciousness, his vision suggested, was to be the next frontier of the tech sector, and Enlightenment Labs would do it virtuously. His conviction only mounted as we talked. And I felt his ambition was birthed from a pure place.

Inspired, I started to open up about my own self-exploration, my attempts to understand *me*. I came clean about *Vivid & Vague*, a blog I'd been quietly writing for the last three years, a sort of philosophical diary that was less about garnering feedback from anyone and more about getting out of my own head, skin, and past, I told him. Sevi said he'd read some of it and had feedback, if I was interested to hear it.

What initially felt like a business interview started to toe the line of a therapy session. While I'd held out for so long, it felt like this was the right person to finally talk to about these things. Not because I pegged him as someone who'd really listen — everyone fucking *listens* — but because he thinks about what he listens to, he does something about what he hears.

I sat across from him and spoke confidently. "Here's the thing. I've been trying to calm my brain down, to quiet the interference. I know there's no real value in analyzing every situation, no reward in creating a puzzle that isn't really there. But I do it obsessively, almost like an addiction. And it can be excruciating, man. It's like a perpetual urge to break things down with thought, to reduce them to their primal elements to understand the working parts — as if life were a mechanical system."

Sevi nodded, asking for more without saying a word.

"Yet I know it's not. I've experienced flow. Problem is, just when I seem to get it, I slip back into this, you know, default mode of analysis. It's exhausting. Sometimes I wonder, is there living and breathing on the other side of this math? It's like I'm continuously building the equation

45

that I'm trying to solve."

Sevi looked at me with a magnetized glare, arresting my vision and focus. Clearly galvanized by my candor, he replied, but did so calmly, mellifluously. I listened, surprised I had discovered a preacher in this strange man but delighted by the truth of his alternative gospel. "Fear is like energy. In fact, it is energy," he said. "I think we can measure progress in relation to, or in units of, fear. The first level is identifying it, feeling its presence everywhere, sensing fear as the omnipresent source. We've reached a breakthrough now, using technology to do this, reducing it to a calculation, binary bits."

I had questions but knew he would explain.

"This thing over here," he said, raising an open palm, "this gets coded as a high-probability trigger." The other hand lifted to represent the opposite, another thing. He looked at it. "That doesn't."

"Got it," I said, to let him know I was tracking.

"Level two is calling for its destruction — promising yourself that you will conquer fear, abolish it from your life, dig deep, and clip fear from its roots," he said. "This happens by setting commitment targets, charting progress, using life data points to learn and improve along the way. It's not that we can't win without digital tools; it's just that our strategy is flawed. We are fighting fire with fire, plunging headfirst into a war with fear because we are afraid of it. We've felt it creep into our bones and blood, we hear it in our words and the voices of our friends. We want to end it because it is a threat, an immediate and pervasive threat to the good in our being, the light. But to make a change, we need an objective scorekeeper as a guide.

"The fight that many of us go through is valiant, I think, but the end goal to rid ourselves of fear is unattainable. We've got to abandon that fight and instead realize the value of fear as a form of energy. After all, energy cannot be destroyed, Andersen. It's got to be harnessed and converted. This is all my personal philosophy, of course. However, I funnel much of that into this business, into the future of Enlightenment. Our mission is to guide people, to provide an intelligent, empathetic system that draws on their experience and directs them toward better decisions and better experiences."

He paused and spun his chair to look out at the skyline. In that quiet moment, I felt myself lightly bobbing my head in consensus, which I may have been doing incessantly while he talked.

Rotating back toward me, Sevi picked up where he'd left off. "Would you like to join us on that mission?"

I'm feeling really good right now because I've found the elusive enzyme that converts inspiration into optimism, and I've successfully harnessed that little fucker.

We are not alone. There are going to be tools that help us do this, that help us cope and thrive and feel happy, and that realization has changed my outlook. We're entering a new era of understanding. For the first time, we're going to make information work for *us*, not just logistically or commercially. We're putting it to work on the development of our humanity.

PART TWO

6

In our kitchen, the refrigerator hummed. Photographs and little mementos clung to its off-white face, lending personality to the big, dumb appliance. Every so often, I would glance at it while enjoying a morning coffee or an evening drink and reflect on the life I had lived, strewn before me like an exposed time capsule.

There was an article profiling Sevi, clipped from the *New York Times*, which reported on the massive Series C round of funding for Enlightenment Labs and lauded its futurist founder. My dad had highlighted a section of the article that mentioned my involvement as VP of Insights, part of Sevi's leadership team. He sent me the clipping on my twenty-seventh birthday, along with a note expressing how proud he was.

Pictures covered most of the fridge. One showed my sister and me in the back seat of our family's car, on our way to my first college move-in day, waiting in a line of traffic outside the Holland Tunnel. Sitting in that Toyota

53

Land Cruiser, surrounded by heaps of shit my dad and I had packed in the night before, I had consciously noted a turning point in my life. I vividly remember the drive and the overwhelming emotion of that day. My mind was so fogged up that I could practically feel the moisture with every thought, the early morning grayness and drizzle mimicking my blurred state. As my life on wheels barreled toward New York City and then merged into the dark tunnel, my brain finally generated its first lucid thought of the day: *Holy fuck.*

An eighteen-year-old freshman, and this was it — my second umbilical cord was about to be cut. We're all born with two, surely: the one the doc offs after we slide out of our utero studio apartment, and the other invisible connection we have to our parents through which they feed us guidance, maybe a little bit of money, lots of bullshit, and love. Now, I'd realized during that drive, I would have to feed myself.

Those first few days and weeks at college kind of had the feeling of a first blowjob — it was fucking great and new and liberating, but it could be a bit toothy at times. There were some kinks to work out, adjustments to be made to manage the sensory overload. First times tend to have that unique quality to them, though, and make great memories for that exact reason. Adaptation is at work, growth in progress. The struggle makes it all worthwhile. Plus, a little bit of tooth never hurt anybody.

My favorite photo on the fridge was taken in

Montreal's Parc La Fontaine, just after I had asked Nina to marry me. One bright September day, I skipped out of the office early, picked her up at her work studio for a surprise trip and shot up route 87, trying to concentrate on the road while drafting a proposal in my head. There was something encouraging and gravitational about heading north, as if the car were polarized and pulled toward positive change, a border crossing. That picture was the image that formed in my head whenever I tried to visualize happiness.

It's comforting to look back on the souvenirs of good times, but for some reason, my eyes always locked onto the graduation card. The *weird* times. The card was a portal to the moment I first sensed an inexorable change within myself, like the last detail you recall from a dream before waking. And I needed the visual reminder. I couldn't remember shit otherwise. My memory was not deteriorating, however; it had always been the least developed department of my brain. Nina often joked about it to mask underlying concern, her trepidation that she may be marrying a liability, creating history with a man who was prone to forget it all. I tried to explain to her that it was a case of never having rather than one of uncontrollable loss.

Here's my theory: If you do not load a given experience with emotion as it occurs, the experience fails to embed itself in the terrain of your mind. All of this is unconscious, of course. I didn't choose what to let in or out, nor did I lack for emotion. For whatever reason, though, I grafted few feelings onto my cerebral cortex to be appreciated later as memory. I simply released them like sweat, content to let the animations of the mind evaporate instead of solidify within myself. Precious clips of the past were not deleted from my memory; I just never created a cache at all.

In the absence of total recall, the fridge and its smattering of magnets did their part to hold tokens of the past in my current view. While the photo from Montreal shined as a portrait of happiness, the graduation card evoked the dire scene I imagined after first reading it — one of a derailed train and its confused conductor, a man who had trouble switching as the tracks ahead diverged.

After college, terrified of unemployment, I joined my peers on a pilgrimage to unfulfilling work. Through three years of swirl in the job market as a freelance writer and advertising strategist, I learned an important lesson about the nature of work and what work *means*. The idea of a vocation, of satisfying demand for one's inward calling out in the marketplace, is pretense; conversely, vocations create value in the opposite direction, outward-in, allowing those who are so lucky to vocalize their attainment of stability and mollify a disturbing sense of instability that's rattling around on the inside. The paycheck is modern society's spiritual life support, and damn, it's good to hear that metronomic beep, wonderful to suck from the hanging IV bag of liquidity that is in such short supply.

In those early years of searching for a meaningful career, my standards were very high. Too lofty, maybe. I wished my paycheck to arrive in tandem with currency for my mind, ideas that I could feel good about. I wanted direct deposit to my checking account as well as the bank that held my moral and philosophical trust. Unlikely, and yet one night I met Sevi at a party, engaged in a bizarre discussion about the information latent in a home bookshelf, and was drawn into his vision for Enlightenment Labs. Moving past my initial incredulity, I realized that his ambitions meshed with my dream of investing time in innovation for good — commerce for a cause. We were going to offer a path to true happiness through technology.

Sevi initially hired me as a planner, a role that was, in many ways, similar to my previous position in advertising. I joined a small team of co-planners and helped develop the practice. We were responsible for cultivating insights, through research into the behaviors of certain segments of users, to inform optimal design of the product. Throughout the beta phase, our research proved invaluable; the engineering team leaned on our reports to guide their software updates, which improved user experience and feedback accuracy, ultimately attracting more customers. Meanwhile, Tway joined the company as a full-time quality assurance tester and eventually rose to lead a QA crew, as they were called. The user base grew rapidly, and Sevi acknowledged my contributions, quickly promoting me to VP of Insights.

In this new role, I took on greater responsibility for the algorithm that steered our main product, the Happiness Engine™. The Happiness Engine™ was the in-market manifestation of the vision Sevi first shared with me when we met at Tway's party. It led the charge of an emergent personal data mining industry. Users would opt in to the service, granting Enlightenment access to their suite of data streams, which could include anything from social networking activity and search history to updates tracked from an online dating app. The engine would churn through this data to uncover patterns that may otherwise be undiscoverable by human awareness, then exercise that information to make recommendations for life choices.

At the time Enlightenment Labs launched the Happiness Engine™, competitors were materializing from all angles. What was yesterday a nascent field quickly became a crowded commercial arena. Sevi predicted this, and our investors wisely predicted his ability to predict — and to pivot. We were backed by the best, flush with cash and staffed with a team of young tech acolytes, making the short commute each day to the alter of innovation. Sevi employed his meditative confidence to motivate the team to blaze a trail into the future.

Like Sevi, a man of dual genius, a sort of cross between Steve Jobs and Carl Jung, Enlightenment's personal data mining application was distinguished on two levels:

1) Unparalleled data contextualization and deep learning.

The Happiness Engine™ built on the progress of algorithmic technology that came before it, namely mainstream applications that pioneered recommendation automation: If you like this, you'll like that, and oh, these friends who share similar interests like this, so you should try it too. Enlightenment achieved this on a grander scale by developing an intelligence that could identify significant correlations across disparate contexts (i.e., beyond the bounds of the social graph and in-app usage patterns). This capability grew out of experimentation around hypothetical questions posed by everyone on the planning team. Can software understand how a change in one space of life influences another? What if a program could not only predict the items you're most likely to be interested in but also map the reasons for one's purchases to certain macro or cultural cues, such as current political events, the state of the economy or personal finances, or one's exposure to a particular work of art?

We benefited from the gift of perfect timing. As our teams at Enlightenment started considering these questions, the Internet of Things reached a tipping point, giving rise to a universal connectedness of teeming devices. Everything from phones to apparel pulsated with data, measuring our world and dropping endless bits of clues about our behavior. Our engineers invented new ways to capture this data and convert it to knowledge.

2) Artificial intelligence fueled by user calibration and emotion analysis.

As life teaches us, intelligence is an unstable currency, susceptible to instant devaluation in the face of any of the universe's many secrets. A whisper of wind rustles your hair into your cheek, the feeling of a delicate touch, distorting your conception of what's real, what's actually there. One moment you think you know, and the next you are unsure of your ability to truly know anything, your whole being trivialized.

Historically, machine learning technologies suffered from the same dilemma. Systems could develop foundations of intelligence but lacked functions of intuition and especially empathy. Again, Enlightenment found a way in. The Happiness Engine™ was built to be smart and *compassionate*. It could form a relationship with the user, sensing implicit indicators as well as acting on direct feedback.

In addition to the streams of digital interaction data, such as what type of content you "like" on social media or what you purchase through an e-commerce portal, the Happiness Engine™ analyzed emotion and private thoughts by probing users with direct questions. For example, you may be prompted by a notification on your phone, asking you to reply: How are you feeling right now? The engine posed questions with deep knowledge of the subtext of your situation (e.g., you're on vacation in Portugal, waking up to a sunny 84-degree day). Where do you want to be one year from now? (You're in Red Hook, Brooklyn; there's $107 left in your checking account; and you just updated your LinkedIn profile.)

Essentially, the Happiness Engine™ conducted constant data- and language-based conversations with users, automating psychoanalysis. It was a great listener, and when it talked back with advice, users listened in turn. Communication passed through a simple and fun-to-use interface, which served up recommendations for life decisions in real time and presented benchmarks for progress through a tracking scale called "Happiness Levels." A new mode of therapy was born.

Each week brings more interaction with my Happiness Engine. We're "talking" to each other quite frequently now. And I sense that friends and family are starting to catch on, asking me questions about what I do at work or what this thing we built does that's so great. Even a few of you who read this blog have messaged me about it. While our internal hard data confirm rapid growth over the last three quarters, I'm just now feeling the public interest mounting. That's exciting.

For those curious, here's a sample of the prompts I've received from my Happiness Engine in the last few weeks, along with my responses. I like to feed it honest but offbeat answers to see how well it deals with conceptual responses and associative thinking.

HE: *Is there anything in your life you would you like to reduce or eliminate that you're having trouble parting with?*

happy, technically.

Me: My ego. I know it needs pruning, but I just find ego too interesting to let go. Can't clip it — not fully, at least.

HE: *Ask me a question that keeps you up at night or deeply puzzles you.*
Me: What is the relationship between our lies and our creativity?

HE: *How do you feel about your life at the moment? Today, right here and now. Use the words "good" and/or "bad" in your response.*
Me: Life isn't good or bad, it's just exhausting.

HE: *Describe your feelings about failure — what it represents to you or how you are affected when you fail.*
Me: I think man is a self-fertilizing animal; we rise up out of our own shit or not at all.

HE: *How would you explain love to someone who has never experienced it?*
Me: Love is like a strike to the funny bone — you don't see it coming and then, all of a sudden, there's an electrical storm inside of you, peculiar chills and tingles enlivening you, followed by a mild pain, a dull hurt.

7

Over the course of three years at Enlightenment Labs, my life accelerated toward true happiness. My career fast-tracked, I developed a well-defined sense of purpose, and I married the love of my life. The fallout of my early twenties — the overwhelming restlessness and solipsism — felt far away, like an abandoned quarry I had once mined for the resources to build a better self. Things had changed for me, not as I'd planned but as I'd hoped, however vague those hopes had been.

I thrived because I loved my work and because the company provided a support system, in terms of both Enlightenment's people and the product itself. As I worked day in and day out on advancing the Happiness Engine, I also became a loyal user. I interacted with the app regularly when it prompted for feedback, and I understood how it mapped my qualitative input onto a structure of facts: locations, times, biometrics. The idea of life methodically surveyed as clusters of data points comforted me. My own analysis would be much messier.

Over time, I granted the Happiness Engine access to more and more of my digital stream, from my Twitter account and browser history to my online investment brokerage and wearable health tracker. It learned what I was watching and reading, how I reacted to cultural events in real time, and how my money and health fluctuated at each turn. Fully aware that more data would enable a higher fidelity, a more feature-rich experience with the software, I was still continuously impressed by how well it performed. Within the first year, I started to heed much of the Engine's lifestyle advice, such as when to take a moment to express gratitude, how to optimize my diet, when to go on vacation. By year two, I was making significant decisions based on automated recommendations: the decisions to ask for a raise, to move to a new neighborhood in a specified borough, to not attend the funeral of my estranged grandfather.

Not being an insider, Nina was naturally more skeptical of the Happiness Engine and hesitated to cede decision making — or "elements of her conscience," as she put it — to an artificial intelligence. In fact, on numerous occasions, she overruled recommendations that I was willing to accept, often sneering, if not playfully, at my guileless trust in technology.

But it wasn't long before Nina converted into a semi-consistent user herself. Results don't lie. While neither she nor I would ever fully attribute our success to the software, we were in a great place, growing happier together and moving toward our big dreams of purchasing a home and having a baby. The job of interpreting meaning was outsourced; we were free to live rather than analyze and speculate.

This period in my life was also enriched by profound relationships beyond family and old friends. On a joint mission to build a life-changing technology, my team and I coalesced into a tight unit of trust and collaborative energy. I led the team with great respect for their dedication and our collective output. Tway was not only a longtime friend but now a true confidant, inside and outside of the office. We went way back and now pushed forward, friends with a rich history and a thirst to make more memories together.

Sevi was a mentor to all of us. We knew there was something special about him — many things, probably — and we relished the opportunity to watch him work or simply pick his brain because it inspired us. He wasn't a boss; he was a guide. He would help us transcend.

A journalist once wrote that Sevi took a "curiously subtle" approach to leadership, but Sevi would argue that personal and career growth are matters of belief and energy (not force and consequence), and that the power of his leadership style lay in the sustainability of it all. He spent a ton of time with his managers on the intangibles rather than operations planning or technical training. What others might call soft skills to him were the elemental

happy, technically.

structure of a successful enterprise. He knew that people building software must bring more to the table than rules and structure, that people need to do more than function according to directions and principles — because that's exactly what software does. And so, what people need to do is conjure a philosophy.

On the first Friday of each month, all director-level team members gathered in Sevi's office to do the conjuring. These meetings lasted half of the day and were legendary for their intensity. A heaviness would fill the room each time, though it wasn't a formality or bureaucracy that weighed down on us, as you would expect from a management meeting; it was a thickness that cooked up as we openly theorized about technologies, stress-tested each other's worldviews *du jour*, and incubated ideas that reached far beyond work (but always related back to the big work we were doing). Sevi called these meetings Monthly Meditations. Each session followed a three-part agenda:

1. Management briefing: Sevi would kick things off by sharing an update of our recent progress, in terms of the company's financial health or other indicators measuring our product-market fit; he'd clue us into any suggestions or directives he'd received from the board, related to financial stewardship or otherwise; and he'd close with an impassioned but intimate expression of his own ideas as CEO, a briefing straight from the source. Sometimes his tone would turn playful, almost mischievous, as he

68

outlined a new idea or new pathway to a standing objective, like an older brother huddling the neighborhood kids to hatch a new game plan. At other times, his briefings were more stoic and chant-like, repetitions of our company values and reinforcements of his long-term vision. He was our older brother and our prophet. Occasionally, the briefing would focus on a particular department or a team's technical challenge, though this was rare. There was an unspoken understanding that we met to synthesize potential big breakthroughs, not to scheme tactics or troubleshoot.

2. Inspirations and philosophies: The second portion of these sessions was used to inject external thinking into our process. Ahead of each Monthly Meditation, Sevi would send the directors an open-ended survey, soliciting topics for discussion and debate. What should we meditate on this month? What could stimulate new thinking or shake us free from the status quo and bad habits? The only rule was that each discussion topic (we called them "prompts") cover either an inspiring new advance in a technology adjacent to our business or an underappreciated field of psychology or philosophy. Our job was to find out why these things might matter to our mission. Sometimes, we determined that they did not matter in any practical or commercially viable terms — but the discussion itself always mattered. The whole purpose of considering these prompts, whether or not they led to actionable ideas, was to hedge against complacency. One

meeting saw us debating the institutional adoption of cryptocurrencies and, shortly thereafter, considering how Heidegger's famous concept of thrown-ness might help us understand how to steer people toward happier states.

3. Brainstorming: The remaining time of each Monthly Mediation was reserved for free-form idea generation. The brainstorms were not led by anyone in particular and tended to be a bit frenetic, but if there was any objective, it was to triangulate an idea or set of ideas by considering some intersection of the three themes we'd pored over throughout the meeting: the state of the company, an emergent or adjacent technology, and a provocative theory about consciousness or the human experience.

One recent Friday, things played out differently. The Monthly Meditation was not a collaborative effort. Instead, as soon as we got started, Sevi let us know he had an important update and he'd be holding the floor for a while to bring us up to speed.

From the minute Sevi started talking, I sensed something unusual about his delivery. He was always intense, so that's not what threw me. Some would interpret his relentless intensity as a pejorative seriousness, but for him, it was an expression of freedom. I understood this. He spoke for himself, not out of duty to anyone else or to any ideology, and his unique brand of seriousness was a byproduct of passion, never an acquiescence to formality or conservatism.

On this day, though, his words unfurled as protocol; an unfamiliar air of decorum filled the room as he spoke.

"I'm excited to share with you all that today is a landmark day for this company," he began. "I'll explain why, but first I want to take a moment to reflect, together. We've all worked extremely hard — not just to bring our vision into focus but also to continually refine and manifest this vision, legitimizing our pursuit of it. When I started this company, I knew it could grow into something big, but I didn't understand its potential for meaningfulness. I didn't understand that once you are responsible for generating meaning, the responsibility compounds into a new type of pressure, not just to succeed but to serve. Each day that I've stepped into this office since, I've grown more confident in our ability, but I've also had a recurring revelation about how ambitious this project is. Therapy at scale, in a smarter, more empowering, more user-friendly way. We're kind of crazy for doing this, guys! But we've really lived up to the magnitude of it all. We've reached a rare point in the life of a startup — or any company, really — a rare point at which not just the market but also the culture and respected institutions have openly validated our purpose."

Validation? Since when did he care about outside approval? I thought.

"When you build a technology, even if you start out building it for yourself, I believe you end up building it for everyone, in a way — even those who will never use it directly. That's what technology is. It is a contribution to the advancement of society. It is a thrust in the momentum of our evolution. I don't think that's true of just any businesses, though. The advent and refinement of a technology of scale uniquely contributes a new way to experience the world."

What is he getting at? Why all the meta reflection?

"Others have recognized this contribution in our work and have reinforced our sense of purpose: our users, investors, various partners of the last couple of years, and now other businesses. The big news is that we've just closed a deal to join another team, an organization that can add a new scientific dimension to the Happiness Engine to multiply our meaningfulness for the people we serve. We've been acquired by Merck."

What? As I processed his words, a mood of disbelief began to express itself throughout the room, arriving physically. I looked around: Some jaws dropped, some eyes widened, some grins formed. And after a collective moment of silent reaction, a few hands shot up, which never happened in this office. No one ever asked permission to speak.

Sevi scanned the room and acknowledged the hands but still held the floor. "I know there are going to be many questions, and we'll use the rest of the time today to talk through them, but for now I'd like to continue so that I can explain as much as possible upfront."

The hands lowered.

"Thanks, guys. Let me give you some background first. For those who are curious, this deal came together in the last three months or so, but not in haste. Initial talks started late last year when I was approached by a Merck executive at the Machine Learning Leadership Conference. She'd seen my 'Algorithms for Happiness' talk and asked if she could pick my brain. The next night, I joined her and one of her colleagues for dinner. Yeah, I had assumptions about the kind of people they would be, that it would probably be this weird, rigid dinner discussion with a couple of uptight suits. But for most of the meal, we barely talked business. We were more alike than I'd suspected — a small table of futurists.

"I was impressed with the breadth of their knowledge of advanced tech — not just of innovative products but of the emergent fields, processes, and components delivering them — and also surprised by their philosophical curiosity, you know, for pharma lifers. It was clear that they cared about context, about how these advancements impact *life*. Like we do.

"We chatted about machine learning, and they asked how the hell we built a system that can process qualitative feedback the way we do. They'd both been using the Happiness Engine — a full year in for her, about half that time for him — and said the qualitative interaction was the most awesome part of the experience, having their own journals and reflections mined and then responded to. She got so excited about this and, at one point, almost shouted, 'How does it parse my unstructured, emotional ramblings?' Ha! I was having fun by this point. So I indulged them a bit, explaining that our version of psycho-analysis is partially built on established work in the field but also from new theories we've derived from our own data. I hinted that the algorithms upweight user inputs they determine to be repressed, not valued enough by the human user. The engine searches for meaning that's been impugned or forgotten.

"At some point, I started to turn the tables and ask about their projects. What were they doing at this conference? They schooled me on networked experimentation, how it's accelerating the rate of innova-tion in chemistry, and how they sought to automate lab work with artificial intelligence. Then we shared notes on our respective AI efforts and how we planned to build ethics guidance into those systems.

"The business agenda revealed itself right around dessert, when the lead exec told me why we were *really* talking: Her team at Merck had been closely track-ing Enlightenment's progress over the last year, along with a shortlist of other select startups, as part of an internal incubator program. They elaborated on what that meant, what their program charter entailed, and why they were so interested in us. By that point, they'd absorbed one other startup, a team from Oregon engineering sustainable new remedies and consumer materials from mycelium

— mushroom filaments. And now they wanted to put an offer on the table to buy Enlightenment.

"Walking back to my room after the dinner, I was honestly fazed for the first time in a while. There is a lot of responsibility and doubt that comes with growing a company, but however difficult it's gotten along the way, I've never lost confidence that it is a noble, worthwhile journey. The small failures have always felt like precursors of progress. The prospect of selling, though, felt like a burden, a whole new type of uncertainty I'd never experienced before. And even though I knew that a lot still needed to fall into place, that it was certainly possible the deal would never even happen — or, if it did, I wouldn't be alone but would have a team supporting me and backing the move — well, just pondering the decision in that moment felt so lonely.

"I wondered what my Happiness Engine would suggest once I recounted my feelings about this experience as feedback, and that cheered me up because it presented a sort of ridiculous, amazing possibility: that I'd created a technology that could end up advising to sell itself, essentially. The thought relaxed me. But I did have a duty to inform the board of Merck's proposition immediately and to consider it myself with as little personal bias as possible.

"Following our dinner meeting, there was an exploratory conference call and plans made for a meeting with other top executives at Merck. From there, the deal progressed as deals do, through lots of accountants and lawyers. I was there at every step, but the collective will of the board ultimately steered the ship. A preliminary agreement was reached this week; there are just a few details and formalities to work through before closing. And now I'm talking to you. You are the first to know."

Sevi stopped, sighed, and leaned back, but he did not rest — he kept the momentum going before the room could react. "I'm sure most of you are wondering where we go from here. This is the end of an era, not the end of our company as we know it. I want to assure you that all of this will continue, with practically the same teams intact, even down to these Monthly Meditations. In setting the terms of the deal, I required that I be kept on as lead of the Happiness Engine product, with full discretion over my team, within a reasonable headcount.

"I want to remind you all that this is an experiment for Merck too. They will not be able to, nor are they expecting to, shift into software development overnight and mold this business unit into their standard way of working. Not gonna happen. They are relying on us to make this acquisition make sense, and that gives us leverage. It puts us in a position of charting our own course. An exciting position that we're all very familiar with.

"The way I see it, we are now a more advanced, more *enlightened* version of ourselves, sporting unparalleled technology, social understanding, and now a new dimension of technical science competency and resources. It's an amazing opportunity. I'm incredibly proud and inspired — more inspired than ever. Okay, now let's talk. Who had those questions?"

o o o

The meeting ended just after 11:30 a.m., earlier than usual, without the full team discussion and brainstorming. I left the room quickly and texted Tway.

You free? Let's get lunch.

MM over already? he responded.

Yeah, I'll tell you about it.

Too early for lunch, dude, he wrote back.

Coffee. Whatever. Just meet me in the lobby in 10.

I waited for Tway in reception, falling into an oblique piece of furniture, some type of modern take on a couch. The beanbags and Japanese floor cushions were free, but I opted to rest on something that didn't make me feel like a six-year-old. Looking across the large lobby, which held a café, ping-pong table, and a bunch of allegedly happy twenty-somethings, I started to download the details of my denial. The atmosphere of the workspace — the whole premise of the company, really — was a tinge discomforting. Doubts about my career began to crystallize.

Why was this revelation just knocking at the door now? Shouldn't I have seen the signs? There is perhaps nothing more new-agey than a technology startup called Enlightenment, funded by a bunch of future-obsessed angel investors. Even "angel investor" sounded fucking ecclesiastical. I had been invited to board meetings on several occasions, and each time it felt like sitting in a room with the leaders of Scientology. A mix of technological enterprise and an almost religious fervor for innovation. At the time, I was prepared to accept that because I viewed us as an altruistic startup. Now we're going to sell drugs and further the delusion that I was convinced we were working to shut down.

vividandvague.com/blog/entry=119

Today was a weird one. I got some news at work that worried me. My job is safe — it's not a matter of security — but the way I feel about my job and its impact may change. We were told about a new direction for the company, which seems at odds with my personal goals and values. It left me questioning the integrity of my boss; I had always known him to be a difficult, head-strong person, but I also looked up to him and trusted him deeply, for years now.

The news bothered me at first, and after thinking about it for the rest of the day, it still might. However, as I write this, I'm open-ing up to what may lie between my worries and the ambitious course set by those I work for. Perhaps this change doesn't need to be a matter of choosing sides. I like to think of myself as someone who can find progress in compromise.

Most people think in black-and-white and are only accepting of one ideological tone at any given time. They inevitably encounter others who reserve their truth for the inverse (and, of course, only the inverse), and when these two people or groups meet, there is a clash. Few can accept and flourish in the gray area; those who do only see one color and thus don't find that color to be anything other than optimal. In fact, they never think of the gray as a derivative of opposing black-and-white; there are no shades of validity. There just is what is. And the abstractions that come along with that are not discounted as vague but embraced as possibility.

8

On Monday morning, the walk into work felt like any other. I slipped right back into the cycle. White walls, fluorescent light, a fresh week to continue the job.

By Tuesday morning, a cagey vibe hovered over the office. Sevi had yet to make a company-wide announcement – that would come at an all-hands meeting set for the following Monday – but news of the acquisition was already spreading beyond the leadership team. When I'd told Tway, he was shocked about Merck, but, in the moment, his taste for adventure overwhelmed his doubts. "Let's channel our disdain for 'the man' into good ideas for how to use his money," he said.

Despite the growing gossip, I didn't pursue the conversation with others. The workload took precedence over speculation about Enlightenment, and the week passed quickly.

When Friday rolled around, it came with an abrupt start. Nina squeezed my arm, rousing me from a dream. I heard myself grunt something unintelligible.

"You're breathing really heavy and mumbling," she said. "You okay?" Her head sank into the pillow, one eye open to scrutinize my reaction. The earliest morning light illuminated her face, which showed a thin mixture of expression, like a martini of seven parts sleep, one part concern. In all the years we had lived together, this was a first. I was a light sleeper but never had nightmares, never felt vulnerable to my dreams.

"Yeah, I'm fine," I said. "Sorry."

She fought to hold the one eye open, maybe to verify that I was being truthful, but gravity won.

I reached for my phone and checked the time: 5:44 a.m. About an hour ahead of the alarm. I figured I wouldn't get back to sleep, and a rising anxiety bubbled in my chest to scare off even the possibility. The sun was coming up and so was a strain of internal fear, from an unknown source, but strong enough to push me to the wrong side of the bed at some point in my sleep.

I rolled out of bed, put on sweatpants, and laced up my sneakers for a run. A few mornings each week, I'd start the day by jogging down to the park to get my blood flowing but rarely this early. I wanted to run off the anxiety and think about why the world wanted me awake. When you get stirred, sometimes the only thing that feels right is to stir back.

I ran below an ambiguous sky. Thick cloud cover held back miles of constrained light as the sun tried hard to find a welcoming entrance. The clouds were collectors, catching dust and holding it above as if to display the debris of something ended in a vast implosion.

My broken-in Nikes carried me a few miles and back to the apartment, away from the portentous heaviness in the cold morning air. At home, I fell into my morning routine: shit, shower, email.

An inbox aggregates our obligations and the myriad reminders that we are not alone: automated billing statements poorly masked by a faux-friendly tone, daily greetings sent from grandma via her new iPad, notifications from everything on the planet that can notify us. My father used to scan newspaper headlines in the mornings, leaving a dust of ink on his fingers, and now I scan these digital subject lines. Severe incongruence or meaningful parallelism? It's hard to tell what's a rabbit hole and what's a portal.

After deleting a few emails, I landed on a familiar subject: "Andersen — Wake Up to Your Weekly Happiness!" An automated note from my Happiness Engine account, scheduled for Fridays. Like many of our users, I looked forward to these for the intel and guidance within but also for the sense of pride they delivered, the firsthand experience of this innovative product, which I helped build, out in the wild. I opened it.

Three lines in and I couldn't believe what I was reading.

o o o

Sometimes, our senses rise to the occasion. The hair on our arms reaches skyward, stiffened by primal awareness, electrified by insight. While the mind ruminates, the body understands. Maybe the most intelligent design is the hardware.

Within minutes of reading the Happiness Engine update, I was dressed and running toward the subway, my present reality an expression of pure reflex. I didn't even say goodbye to Nina.

I had to talk with Sevi, in person, immediately. The email must have been sent in error. Maybe the engineers were fine-tuning an algorithm and something bugged, a database went dark, or the natural language processing lacked a critical update. Just a digital hiccup. I would rush in and confirm the mistake.

Of the many steps descending into the subway station, I touched only three or four. More reflexes followed: wallet out, Metrocard swiped, turnstile cleared. Then weaving through fellow commuters. In another context, they are people. Here, they are fleshy obstacles of different shapes and sizes. I clutched my laptop bag in front of me, against my stomach, like a running back. Cutting laterally, then forward; laterally, then forward again. In desperation, I am the Barry Sanders of the New York City underground.

happy, technically.

My feet, trained by days, weeks, months, and years of the same commute, kept on course. Spotting an open-doored train, I accelerated and made it just in time, coolly enjoying one of the tiny pleasures a brutal city can yield. The doors closed and the train pushed away from the platform toward Manhattan. The surrounding darkness invited the equally dark confusion in my mind to swirl as the train tunneled below the East River. My job and my personal life were clashing in a battle royale that threatened my sanity, and I was leading the armies on both sides.

o o o

I surfaced on the blacktop about twenty minutes later. The sun, still constrained, shot darts into the city without delivering any palpable warmth. Cold air pushed at my back as I moved through the building's revolving door and nodded to Jay, the security guard, who watches faces pass for a living and may have noticed mine was full of worry. In the elevator, I held my breath as if lightening myself would speed up the ascent.

When the doors parted, I stepped out into the foyer, keycard already in hand to swipe at the office door. Inside, Lex was just settling in.

"Sevi here?" I asked.

"Yep," she said. "And good morning."

Already past her, I raised a hand in thanks.

I found Sevi in his office, baked into the mold

85

of routine, his feet up on the desk and iPad in his lap. I knocked twice on the glass door but didn't wait, sliding it open.

"I need to talk to you," I said, demanding my right to time and space for a conversation.

He picked up on my seriousness, meeting it with genial opposition. "First thing in the morning? This must be special. How about you talk *with* me," he said, smiling but without breaking concentration on the device. Never willing to cede control, this guy. He always found a way to wrench a situation in his own vice.

This time, I refused the pressure, denied the terms. My world was term-less now. A fucking email shattered the terms. I needed to know if what we built — if what I helped this genius develop — was actually a system for progressive life-hacking, the next step in the evolution of human insight, or if it was simply a shiny technological vice of control, clamping my life and the lives of our users into the hold-still grip of conformity that profit can pounce on.

"Tell me why the Happiness Engine is challenging the best thing in my life," I said. "It's not right. There's a glitch."

"Andersen, slow down. You're clearly upset, but we'll work this out, I'm sure. Let's just be calm. First of all, you know as well as I do that it's not wrong. If it makes you happy, we'll check the feedback logs at the end of the day, see if there's a rise of any statistical significance, something that may suggest a system error. It's much more likely that *you* are wrong, though, rather than the engine."

My eyes wandered to the window as he spoke, but I listened for every word. Cloud cover still obstructed the skyline. The view outside the room offered no more clarity than our conversation within it.

"It's chewing on the data and giving you a decisive point of view," Sevi said. "Whatever the recommendation, it's the best one possible, given the inputs. This I know. But I'm curious — what are we talking about here? What's the best thing in your life?"

As if he didn't know me. As if, when we talked, when we connected as humans, he didn't sense the inflection in my voice or see the change in my body language or hear the words I used when talking about *her*. Maybe he just didn't know love, had no direct experience of being in a relationship like mine, had no exposure to the power and cogency that come with unconditional friendship, meaningful sex, shared triumphs and disasters, shared time. He was not fortunate enough to live it and therefore did not know it, could not recognize it out in the world, something outside of himself.

I didn't want to engage him in a test of empathy, though. I served it to him straight. "My update this morning recommended that I leave my wife." I shuddered as the words traveled from my mouth and crossed the desk between us.

"Well. Oh, man," he said, unhooking his feet to sit

upright. He placed the iPad on the desk. "I'm sure that was hard to read. I can tell you're gutted. Have you received any updates related to this before?"

"No, this is completely unexpected. Out of nowhere."

"Okay, listen. I know this is hard. But again, it's never out of nowhere. The engine is acting on signals and patterns. You and your team have actually interviewed individuals and couples to help inform exactly this sort of thing, the software's response to a failing relationship. You know this. I have no idea what's triggering the recommendation in this case, but it very well could be originating from your own insight."

"Sevi, I hear what you're saying. But there's got to be a mistake. I'm extremely happy with Nina, deeply in love. I have never provided feedback to my engine to suggest otherwise."

Sevi sighed audibly — a telegraph of frustration. "Your view of love is quixotic, Andersen. The technology is simply breaking through that idyllic surface. I know it's not so simple, but you should embrace this because it's exactly what we've been trying to do all along. Get people to open up to what can be harsh truths in exchange for an empirical view of their lives."

"No. This is fucked," I said. "Not just my situation, but if — if the Happiness Engine is making calls like this, disrupting social dynamics, you know, tearing down relationships based on inferences, then it's edging too far. We need to step it back."

Sevi shrugged and leaned back in his chair again. "There's no going back, man. We've built it. And there's nothing optimal about the past. It's not a place you can ever get to, anyway. It seems that the problem with you, and me, and all of us, really, is that we create a very strong, false association between reality and everything that once was."

He continued to lecture. I listened but pored over an alternative set of facts in my head, including thoughts of overzealous innovation, pharmaceuticals prescribed by machine learning software, a digital system extending its reach into the real world, the tangible. "You're here, living in the now, where you've been given the gift of new information," I heard him say, though the words were beginning to flatline. "It may be unexpected news, but that doesn't mean it's suboptimal. And if you continue to feel unhappy, despite now knowing *why*, well, maybe it's within you, beyond the engine's influence. Maybe it's chemical —"

I put my hand up to stop him. I'd received all the new information I could take. He stopped talking but persisted with his stare, continued the conversation through eye contact. A few long seconds passed before I broke the connection and showed myself out.

This time, I did not rush. Nothing to hurry for. My legs did not work as they had earlier, when adrenaline called the shots. Instead, I drifted as one does when each new step is in question. I left the building immediately and parked myself in a coffee shop two blocks away, a place I'd sometimes go to take a break from the office. Ordered a cappuccino, stowed away in a booth, and flipped open my laptop. On impulse, I began transferring personal documents and deleting various notes and data, an attempt to clear my presence from the device. I figured I would not be employed by Enlightenment for much longer.

I muted my team's chat channel and set a vague auto-response for email. I did not check my Happiness Engine but thought about contacting Sevi to see if, just maybe, he'd heard back from the engineers about a glitch. Yet, I knew the chances of an error were slim. Paralyzed by epiphany, I spent the rest of the morning in limbo, bouncing from one café to another for caffeinated melancholy and free Wi-Fi.

At some point, I began to write. I started on a new blog post, then moved on to a long piece that occupied me for hours. It hit the page in a different shape than my typical journal entries, arriving as narration; the process of questioning my love, my career, and my purpose disguised as story. It helped me feel a bit better.

Just after 5:00 p.m., I broke my concentration and sought fresh air. I'd spent almost a full work day writing. Stepping out onto the street, the darkness caught me off guard. Streaks of yellow came into relief against a black city and blackening sky, the occasional taxi whizzing by in protest of its own extinction. Sometimes, New York can truly be the most confusing, depressing place on earth, and tonight, my gears painfully grinding along the streets of Tribeca, it was. Moments later, I disappeared into a dive bar around the corner. Lost.

The place was busy but not yet packed. Beer gushed from cold kegs and weakness flowed freely throughout the crowd. The music was loud and good, but not transcendent; good like a kiss on the cheek is good. Sidestepping a group of friends, I found a stool at the near end of the bar and plopped down. I felt my cynicism percolating and wanted to drown it with a drink. The bartender caught my stare and beat me to it.

"What can I get ya?"

"Bourbon on the rocks, please," I said.

"You got a favorite?" she asked.

"Uh, let's do Wild Turkey. And when you have a second, I'd like to ask you something."

She'd heard that one before. "Yeah, all right," she said, then turned and slid a few yards down the bar to search the array of bottles.

She returned quickly, an accomplice to the Wild Turkey habit I had inherited from my dad. Her brief, dismissive eye contact confirmed that my offer of conversation was off the table. I would deal — it wasn't her I was interested in. I just needed a face to talk at, anything with a heart and a brain. A soul in a body, not a database in the cloud.

She poured quickly but carefully, then grabbed for my credit card on the counter. "Keep it open?" she asked.

I raised the glass, a cheers to her offer.

After a few pensive swigs and a minute of vapid people-watching, my thigh began to buzz. I reached into my pocket for my phone, a sleek slab of glass and plastic that harnessed streams of consciousness, saving thoughts from disappearing into the ether without due recognition. Everyone in the bar had a similar device, just as they had all grown up with a beloved blanket, or, at the very least, a thumb to suck on.

It was Tway: *You leave the office yet?*

I wrote back in clicks, the modern Morse code. I was in the trenches and needed reinforcements. *Yeah. At a bar. Meet me for a drink.*

Buzz. *Sounds good. Need about 15 mins to finish at work. You near the office? Which bar?*

It dawned on me that I had no idea. Looking up from my phone, I searched for someone I could ask, but everyone else at the bar was paired up with a friend, a lover, or their phone. The bartender, who'd been shaking cocktails while talking to a coworker at the other end of the bar, came back my way to stop at the register. I flagged her with a quick raise of one arm and both eyebrows.

"Another one already?" she said.

"What's the name of this place?" I asked.

"What?"

"What's the name of this bar?"

"You really do need someone to talk to, don't you?" she said.

"I've got a friend coming to meet me, except he doesn't know where I am, and neither do I. But yeah, I would like someone to talk to."

"Okay," she said. "I'm all ears. But don't think I'm rude when I walk away. I've got to keep my other customers happy too."

I nodded.

"You're at The Belgian, by the way. Couldn't you have just shared your location with him?"

"Thanks," I said, ignoring her question to look back down at the glow emanating from my palms. It begged for my attention and I answered it. *The Belgian,* I wrote to Tway.

"Is this about love?" the bartender asked.

I looked up, startled by her question. She hovered closer than before, resting both hands on the bar and leaning my way.

"The person meeting me? No. He's just a friend," I said.

"Not him," she said. "You wanted to ask me something. Is it about love?"

"Why would you assume that?"

"Listen, you come into a bar alone for one of two things. Either you're hoping to find love or you've just lost it."

"First of all, I'm not here to be alone," I said. "And second, maybe I came in for the TV."

She smiled, the first one she'd let through since I'd

been there, a crack in the hardness of her presence. Over her right shoulder, above the stock of backlit booze, little figures glided across a screen. I loved hockey but hated bars with TVs.

"All right, I didn't come here to watch anything," I said.

"Right," she said, and turned to grab the Wild Turkey. She refilled my glass. Then, reaching down, she pulled a clean one from behind the bar and poured a couple fingers for herself.

"Listen. Being in love, in some complex relationship, the whole devotion thing . . ." She paused to gulp the neat brown drink. "It's just a way to feed your ego."

I treated myself to another sip. "I think it can be the opposite. Maybe it's a surrender, a recognition of the fact that no one else on the planet really gives a fuck about me or can understand my weirdness, so my ego has only the value of one, ascribed by this relationship."

She stared straight at me, hands still clasped on the bar's edge, two kickstands for her lean. "Shit, you've really thought it out, haven't you?" she asked. "Look, if you want to settle down, be my guest. No one's stopping you."

"He *is* trying to stop me," I mumbled.

"The guy coming here?"

"No. And yeah, it is about settling. But you shouldn't take the beauty out of that."

The bartender slid away, unfazed by my stink of sadness. She had heard it all before, all types of heartbroken bullshit, and she served the sauce to foment plenty more. Maybe it paid her rent throughout college. Financed her student loans afterward. And, eventually, it crept up on her as a comfortable career.

My burgeoning young career had dropped in my lap by way of a chance meeting at a party in Brooklyn and was about to vanish just as quickly. My employer and my mentor, Sevi, was questioning the best thing in my life. And not only was I affiliated with the source of this contradiction, but I directly influenced it. I decided then and there, in that downtown dive, that I didn't want to *find* meaning, or generate it, or classify it in an orderly fashion. I wanted to be inundated by it, to hack my way out of it like a machete-wielding madman in a lush rainforest, the thicket of life.

Our thoughts and the record of them should invite reflection and inspire new thought, not confirm boundaries and definitions based on the originals. By quantifying thinking and feeling, the Happiness Engine mythologized early versions of the user's own consciousness, setting baselines and benchmarks that, outside of the rules of the application, had no real bearing on the world or lives lived within it. And what Sevi now proposed, a pharmaceutical layer, was myth stretched further, synthetic myth. It would be an override of the stories created by the mind and body to hedge against any outliers, anomalies, or subpar experiences.

If the genius of the Happiness Engine was to keep

reflexive self-consciousness in check to promote a template of objectivity, then this pharma deal would be a checkmate, a denial of any value in self, of intuition and storytelling as important aspects of consciousness. In merging data science with pharmaceuticals, the Happiness Engine would compel users to comport with reality rather than feel for its edges, to succumb to reality in its obvious form instead of letting it expand in the fractal patterns that it so beautifully, and confusingly, seems to do. *Rescued by objectivity.* Maybe that's what it meant to be happy, technically.

After a few minutes of working through these thoughts alone, I noticed a peripheral face interrupting my reverie.

"Dude," Tway said.

I turned fully to put him into focus.

"I've been sitting here for like two minutes, watching you stare into your drink. You all right?"

The bartender interjected, grabbing for my almost-empty glass. "Your friend here is concerned about you. And I am too," she said to me.

"Can we get the tab, please?" Tway asked.

"One more," I said, nodding toward the glass. The bartender and I both had our hands on it now, grasping for control.

"Fine. But let me give you some advice if you're going to be in my bar, drinking in sadness. I don't mind the lonesome drinking. It's the sadness that I can't stand. We need some boundaries when it comes to the constant over-sharing of everyone's dissatisfaction with life. We're each trying to work through our own problems here, our own impossible questions, but all the while, we are shelled with the incessant complaints of others. It's like having to plunge someone else's shit-clogged toilet. And I'm over it." With that, she released the glass and turned back toward the bottles.

Tway stared sharply at me — a spear of a look. *What the fuck happened here?* his eyes asked.

I didn't answer, but I didn't wait for the tab either. I dropped a twenty on the bar and walked out.

"What was that all about?" Tway shouted in pursuit. I realized I was speed walking and slowed down. He pulled up beside me, and we embraced.

"Just a rough day in New York, man," I said. "This shit with work, the acquisition. A lot of uncertainty. Sevi and I got into it this morning, and I just bailed."

"Ah, shit. What happened with Sevi? I know, he can be so callous at times, but don't take it personally. I'm sure his heart's in the right place."

Yeah, sure, under his goddamned ribcage, I wanted to say. But I didn't want to get into it with Tway, not all of it, not the whole truth. This was only my business now. Mine and Nina's. I needed to talk to her.

"It's not important. I just overreacted," I said. "I came here to clear my head and I took it out on her, I guess. That bartender."

"Well, Leo just hit me up for drinks. You interested

in a couple more? Wanna take it out on us instead?"

"No thanks, man. Promised Nina dinner tonight."

"All right, let's take a walk then," Tway said, pointing uptown. "I'll drop you at the train on my way."

We headed north and talked about our respective relationships with the city as its rough surface wore down our soles. We knew it so well because we had walked on it and through it for years now. Tway, always a sport, didn't often take a sardonic tone, but tonight he breathed despondence. A couple of cronies, he and I.

"This place," he said, "I used to think it was beautiful, and it *was* beautiful. But I'm getting over it now, I think. Plus, the rent is too damn high." We laughed.

"At least the psychosis is free," I said. We laughed again and it seemed to echo for a long time, down and back West 4th Street. I said goodbye to Tway and took a flight of stairs beneath the city to catch the F train.

I should be at work right now, but I'm not. Had to get out of there and clear my head. I opened up this morning, telling someone in the office about a serious personal problem, a dis-sonance I was sensing between my life and the job. Something — some things, actually — I'd learned very recently that provoked a fount of unhappiness. The conversation did not go well. He rebuked me for insinuating our work was the problem and not a salvation.

"Maybe it's chemical," he said.

Yeah, it's chemical . . . but I'm the fucking chemist. Why should that require a fix from outside of myself?

Come on. How many people have you met who don't have some type of shit-storm raging behind a closed door, their gym routine and brunches and social media just part of a barricade trying to keep that door shut? It may feel really personal to you, reader, like your life just happens to be an especially precarious experience. This

99

happy, technically.

is all of us, man. Icebergs. Thirty percent of us visible, strutting around like we know what the fuck is going on, while the majority of our being is submerged. The real question, once you know that you're an iceberg, is whether you're at peace with it or goddamned furious about the fact that we're also fucking melting, all of us.

Either way, a pill or an app or even a guru is not going to reverse the inevitable.

9

On the train heading home, I thought about Nina. What she might say, how she would react. We had been through this before, me having some life-size revelation and wanting her to understand and validate it, wanting her to say, "Go with it, I love you and trust you," because if she did that meant my sense about the world was not misguided, that my decisions were, in fact, the *right* ones in the grand scheme of things. I mean, if she still loved me, then what else mattered? I must be right on some level. But how much patience for a new belief system or a new career trajectory did she have left? Throughout our relationship, she had always been the steady one, consistent in her vision of the future — our future. My vision flickered at times, becoming visions.

The F jolted to a stop and the doors opened at 2nd Avenue. A gust of cold, chalky air rushed into the train car. The platform was exhaling and, in doing so, spit a few new passengers onboard. An elderly woman pushing a cart led the pack, rough-skinned and weary-looking but confident in her movements. She caught the eye of a man who started to stand and offer his seat, but she waved it off with a quick shake of the head — like a pitcher shrugging off the sign for a pitch that would be too obvious. We'd all seen her before; she was a piece of New York, as native as the pavement and the boulders in the parks and the rusted fire escapes. You see her every day in this city. There was something comforting in the recurring admiration that you might feel for her, but running into her also made you question if you really wanted to stay here *that* long.

Behind her, a crew of four friends shuffled on, talking loudly. College students, probably. They carried an enthusiasm that clashed with the apathy of the end-of-a-long-week commuters. I was drawn to their energy as I heard snippets of their conversation: "ten-dollar cover," "gonna be tight, though," "late-night sesh." That's when we began, Nina and I. In those times, talking about those things, awakening to adulthood but still in those last moments of slumber before your eyes fully open to the real world.

As the train snaked through lower Manhattan and crossed into Brooklyn, I thought about the first time Nina and I met, during junior year. We were at the place of a mutual friend, a girl who'd lived in her dorm the first year but knew me separately through several classes we shared. A bunch of us gathered to drink before going out on a Thursday night, but we never made it to the nearby bar we'd wanted to try. At the apartment, the music was good, most of us were already connected by one degree of separation or less, and the drinks were cheap. Why leave?

My memory of that night is biased because I romanticize it, of course. I recall it in fragments: one moment staring at her lips as they closed gracefully, finalizing an honest thought; another, sitting opposite each other and alone for the first time, her on the edge of a couch and me in a chair, the coffee table a buffer. We sat there smoking a joint, which burned long and slow, to my delight. It gave us a reason to keep talking, lubricated the chatter. Bless whoever rolled that thing. We sunk into our seats and deeper into ourselves.

Unlike every first encounter I'd experienced in my life to that point, particularly with women, I found I needed no extra effort to process Nina's words. I didn't have to reach for anything. Without instigation, her ideas dripped toward me like moisture pulled by gravity. Nina spoke softly and cathartically, and I remember this one thing she said exactly: "I feel like people are trying to kill time because they can't make sense of it, and I'm just not up for that."

Careful not to disturb her train of thought — I understood the fickle nature of such moments of clarity — I didn't ask what she meant, and didn't ask that she reach any further either. We had just met and, if not already in love, I was floored by its potential.

Now, almost a decade later, I walked up the steps

of our brownstone to tell her that a piece of technology
— albeit one entangled in my life on many fronts — was
questioning the validity of our relationship. Bizarre, in a
way, that software would intervene in what had started as
a purely human connection and that I would take it as a
serious affront. There was always the option to keep it to
myself and continue as usual, at least for a little while. Or
fib, spin another story about why I had to walk away from
Enlightenment. But I couldn't just tuck this one away.
It presented too much dissonance, an imbalance that, if
untreated, could spread to every corner of my life: my
career, my relationship, my spirituality.

When I walked in, Nina was chopping vegetables. An uncorked bottle of red wine stood nearby on the
kitchenette table and familiar music filled the room: Neil
Young. A standard Friday night scene, this was her way of
unwinding from a long day, a long week. She didn't notice
me until the door had closed. Now she looked up, and I
could see agitation in her expression.

"Hi, babe," I said.

"Hi," she said, looking down again and continuing
to chop.

"What's up? How was your day?" I moved close
and kissed her on the cheek.

"It was fine," she said, still chopping.

I kept quiet, knowing there was more.

"Actually," she hesitated, "I don't think you said
goodbye this morning, which is weird. And I was trying to

get a hold of you this afternoon. Why didn't you text me or anything?"

"I'm sorry. Had a weird day and needed to unplug for a bit."

"Where were you? I actually got home early for a change. You could have unplugged with me." Nina talked with her hands, unconsciously waving the knife, but there was nothing threatening about her. She would not care that I was out with Tway and spent the evening at a bar. I was a free soul in this relationship, and that's why I was in it. Something else was on her mind.

"I went for drinks with Tway," I said, omitting the part about drinking alone. "Got some unexpected news at work. Everything's fine — I just wanted to relax and talk through it with him since he's close to what's going on."

"No worries," she said. "Let's talk about it in a sec. I just want to finish this first. I have something I want to tell you too."

I watched her transfer the vegetables to a baking sheet before she doused them in oil. She grabbed the pepper mill — *twist, twist, twist* — then gracefully sprinkled some salt with dancing fingers and a fluid wrist, just like a chef. Cooking soothed her, and it was fun to watch.

When Nina finished, she joined me on the couch in the next room, bringing the bottle of pinot noir and an extra glass. She poured herself a glass and then motioned toward mine, but I didn't want to introduce the whiskey to red wine. "I'm good," I said. She wrinkled her nose and poured it anyway.

The music, which had faded to the background of my attention, made an abrupt transition to hip hop, or funk, maybe. The playlist must have turned over. I walked over to the speaker, turned the volume down slightly, and plopped back onto the couch.

"So, I've got something I want to ask you," Nina said, drawing first. "I'm sorry — I want to hear about your day too. I just need to get something off my chest."

"No problem, babe," I said. "Shoot."

She took a deep breath, a yoga breath. "Are you tired of this place at all?" she asked. "Like, how set are you on being here for a long time? What would it take for you to leave?"

"What do you mean? This apartment? This neighborhood?" I remembered there were only about eight weeks left on our lease. "New York?"

"New York," she said, then immediately brought the glass to her lips, staring right at me as she took an expectant sip.

What was this, some kind of test? "What is this, some kind of test?" I asked.

"No," she said, sympathetically. "I'm not testing you, babe. It's a real question. And I've been thinking about it, seriously. That's the news I got today, that I should —" She paused. "That *we* should move on from New York." Nina looked into my eyes, then back down into her glass, where a whirlpool formed as she swirled the wine, letting things open up.

Leaving New York. We'd talked about this many times, casually floating the idea of making a more comfortable life in another place. But she brought conviction to it now, said she was serious, said we *should*. It shook me. Where was this coming from? I was thankful for my wine now and brought it to my lips before I could say anything stupid. I took a slow sip and tried to understand.

Leaving New York.

It didn't register at first, but then, there it was, a shadow of understanding coming into form as fresh light illuminated the source. I brought the wine down from my face. The glass in my hand, it occurred to me, was extremely fragile. Easily broken if I tried to keep too firm a grip on things. I felt duped, and not by the news itself but by the source of it.

Could it be? It had to be: Nina's Happiness Engine.

Of course. Nina had a daily email ritual too; she used apps to guide her experience, she relied on technology. It was *news* to move on from New York — not intuition, not a decision, but an automated message delivered in a regularly scheduled update to her inbox. To think that Happiness Engine news was a singularly disruptive phenomenon for me would be ridiculous. I now knew better.

But what the fuck?

"Andersen," she said, snapping me out of my internal dialogue.

"Yeah." I looked up at her, reengaged.

"Are you okay? I know that was kind of intense to just, you know, drop on you like that."

"No, it's all right. I'm fine. I'm glad you said something. You know it's important to me that we always talk things out."

"I know. Me too," she said. "So what do you think? I know it's kind of out of the blue, but after sitting with it for a while today, it started to feel right to me. Do you feel that at all? Does it make any sense to you?"

"Well, I thought we'd be here for a while. Not forever, obviously. We've always talked about moving on at some point, but it's only been this vague idea. If it's meaningful to you, though, if there's a reason to change things, I'm open to it." I stopped myself for a second to measure how far I wanted to push things. "It was your Happiness Engine, wasn't it?"

She let a smile slip, an admission written in the curl of her lips. "Yeah. I knew you'd know right away."

"Did it say this about *us*, that *we* should move? Or just you?"

"Us, of course. The recommendation was to move beyond this city to give our relationship and my career the space they need to grow."

"Okay," I said. It was all I could summon.

"I'm still a little embarrassed by it, though," she said. "I mean, I know you believe in it, obviously, but I'm not sure how normal it is to get news like that. News that can potentially uproot your life. Seems a little absurd, if I think about where it's coming from. But it does *feel* right. Is that normal, to get serious recommendations like that?"

"Well —" I started to answer, but she cut me off.

"I guess I'm so unsure 'cause I don't have a point of reference for how other people use it. The Happiness Engine, I mean. What kind of guidance do other people get? Do they act on it? You never talk about your Happiness Levels or recommendations."

I nodded. She was right. And I knew it was not an accusatory jab, just a plain statement. She was thinking out loud, but didn't press me any further.

"You don't think I'm weird for taking it so seriously, do you?" she asked.

"Of course not. Many people do. Remember when I was torn up about whether or not to go to my grandfather's funeral? All the family stuff was too murky. I had no feeling of what the right or best thing to do was. I didn't ask for it, but the morning of, my Happiness Update arrived with a recommendation. That was all I needed, some kind of signal from outside myself."

"Oh," Nina said, untethering her eyes from mine to look downward. "I didn't know that." She moved a stray piece of hair away from her face and locked it behind her ear, a subtle defensive posture I'd gotten to know over the years. Maybe it worried her that, after all this time, there were still things we didn't know about each other.

I brought us back to her news. "I'm only surprised because I didn't think you'd even been using your

Happiness Engine much. Or, at least, not enough to get this deep."

"I wasn't for a while. I just couldn't get into the journaling side of it, responding to those automated questions all the time. That stuff never felt authentic to me. Watching you make this abrupt transition to Enlightenment, though, and how you've thrived in your career since, inspired me and also left me wondering what *my* big next step needed to be. At first, I started because I felt like otherwise I might fall behind. Not behind you, but just in general. I mean, we need all the help we can get, right? Seems like everyone's tapping into these apps for an edge. I fell right into that. After a few months, it became less of a conscious thing and more of an urge to understand more about myself and how I can improve. And believe me, I've been happy. And was happy way before this — you've made me so happy. But at times I have felt far from living with real purpose or being my best self."

"Hm," I said, buying myself time to wonder about what she'd been submitting to the software through her journals. Maybe reflections on the state of our young marriage, or anxieties about one day soon balancing a family with her career ambitions — things that were creeping into more and more of our conversations lately. What data triggered the recommendation to leave the city? Were these patterns that I should have seen?

Before we could wade deeper into the issue, the oven started beeping. "Oh, shit!" Nina said, jumping up from the couch. "The veggies."

I watched as she carefully retrieved the tray of roasted peppers, carrots, and eggplant, then turned to the stove. Curls of steam rose from a pot, begging for the ceiling. I hadn't realized other things were cooking, but now the aroma arrived. I'd apparently regained just enough clarity to start processing other senses.

Nina began plating the meal while I sank into the couch, hungry though not fully interested in the food just yet. First, I needed a moment to chew on this situation, to examine the puzzle between us.

The problem was not the Happiness Engine dropping bombshells but the fact that the bombardment lacked coordination. A massive contradiction between Nina's news and mine suggested the software did not grasp how interconnected our lives were. Or maybe it was programmed to neglect this variable to optimize our individual happinesses. Perhaps this is more of a meta issue, a flaw in the pursuit of happiness itself: that the pursuit is inherently egocentric, that happiness as we understand it is not a goal or metric best suited to a networked life of interdependence and tangles.

In that moment, I felt I had stumbled upon something profound but couldn't fully understand it. The mind finally puts a blurry image into focus, and yet, despite its clarity and sharpness, your confusion isn't resolved. That's when the image itself may be the problem, not its resolution.

I knew it was wrong the second the Happiness Engine recommended that I leave her. Whatever actually triggered the recommendation — immature artificial intelligence or subconscious biases exposed by software, a minor glitch or suggestive patterns in the data — it was wrong, and I would override it. When I read that email, my rejection of the recommendation was immediate and absolute. I did not question my reaction or subsequent actions. It had nothing to do with logic; my response was an intuitive one, a definitive self-belief, a defense of conscience and of love. My bone marrow bubbled with this feeling.

I wanted to tell Nina that it was flawed, that she could not fully trust any recommendation. That soon we would see our Happiness Engines point to pharmaceutical solutions, offering happiness as a matter of dependence. That the only option was to unplug.

However, I could not know for her. I could not know for anyone; I had no claim to this as an objective truth. Who was I to call into question another user's experience, their life experience?

Some people have God. I've never had God.

But maybe I have. The God-people have always told me that I *could* have God in my life, that I *should remain open to him,* so it's not unreasonable to consider the possibility that I have been graced with God's presence without initiating contact.

I have certainly had overwhelming good-ness in my life, though, at least tastes of it, pinches of sugar dashed into the complex recipe of my experience.

I have had moments of clarity, indelible moments that appear ordinary in almost every way, all calm on the surface except for a shiver on the skin or a slight dilation of the pupils, but within, there is a change happening; within, there may be a tectonic shift in the soul.

I have listened to music — created by someone else — that is somehow a therapeutic interpretation of the exact emotions that I've desperately tried to unpack, and I have heard in this music chord movements that in themselves are wonderful little magic tricks: gorgeous, elusive sleight of hand performed through sound. I have heard guitars and bass that trudge and crunch like earthen phenomena but at the same time hold the ethereal promises of alien transmissions.

I have emerged from dark subway plat- forms, agitated amid the madness of the morning commute, and, once upon the city surface, I have watched as the sun uses skyscrapers for its mirror, projecting warm, orange triangles onto cold industrial steel, and in those moments I have felt a peaceful oneness with the eight million people who, just seconds before, I was trying to escape.

I have fallen in love with someone and in doing so have realized that I could fall in love with anyone, but that's the point: In learning to love a person, love becomes about loving humanity, not just another self.

But I have not prayed. I have not found a sentience outside of myself that can help me as much as I can help myself from within.

And yet I have been spiritually thankful for all of this, the magic of music and the way that sunlight can melt a cold city down to a soup of striving misfits and the feelings of col- lective love that can stem from one romance. No, I'm not always thankful — not in every moment — but forever thankful and occasionally exploding with enough gratitude to last a lifetime.

happy, technically.

Is that not God? Is gratitude not prayer?

10

That night, Nina and I talked for hours. The bottle of wine, which I did not intend to drink, became two. She brought me up to speed on her evolving relationship with her Happiness Engine, describing recent scenarios in which she'd relied on the app for advice. The recommendation to move was different, though, she said. Of all the updates she'd ever received, this one felt most homegrown, like a bold choice she'd *made*, if not actively or consciously. It gave her a deep sense of optimism.

Eventually, I broke my own news and told her I needed to leave Enlightenment Labs. Sevi and I were running into serious philosophical differences, I explained. Was it something we could work through? she asked. No, I said, today was the last straw.

Nina's raw surprise, which I projected might slip into sour frustration, instead gave way to excitement. In spite of my new joblessness, she homed in on the coincidence we now shared, both of us making big moves that bore opportunities to reset our lives at the same time. Things must be playing out this way for a reason, she said. I did not reveal to her that the Happiness Engine was at the crux of both of our conditions, pointing us in opposite directions.

Nina did ask, with concern, what I'd be giving up financially — a fair question that caught me off guard. I improvised and tried to downplay it, the upside of the equity I held in the company. With an acquisition on the horizon, this worried me too. I would come to recognize it as a small sacrifice, however. Enlightenment, I've found, is a solitary venture, a risk made not to realize a return but rather to realize that you've held onto nothing but conceit for all this time. There is no return of or to anything.

o o o

Later that spring, after the motions that come with resigning from jobs and giving up a lease, we packed up our apartment. It took several days to empty and clean the place. And then we could look at it unadorned, our small cubby in the city also a vast black hole of memories and rent. We decided to throw a spontaneous party that final night.

It was a nice time. I mentioned to Nina that I was glad our friends who showed up outnumbered the boxes. Things change over the years, and I wasn't so sure it would be that way.

The next morning, I again found myself in a car stuffed with all my belongings, inching through New York City traffic. Ten years later, and some of those moving-to-the-city feelings bubbled up. This time, however, I was leaving, and not through a tunnel. We headed north out of Manhattan and crossed the Hudson via the George Washington Bridge.

About three hours into our road trip, we agreed to make a quick stop. With no rest area up ahead, a gas station or fast-food spot would have to do. I aimed the car at the nearest exit, easing off the highway like a pilot peeling away from his wingmen. Leaving the river of brake lights felt contrarian, almost rebellious, but sometimes we break flow for certain needs: Nina had to pee, and I wanted a chance to eat among the people of America.

We got lucky and spotted a standalone restaurant just off the highway. "There!" Nina shouted as a pink neon *Diner* sign came into view, flickering from atop the curved roof of what looked like an oversized chrome trailer. I pulled into the parking lot and chose one of the many empty spaces right by the diner's entrance. Before I could come to a full stop, though, Nina's passenger door flung open and she was halfway out of the car.

"You go ahead," I said, to myself, apparently. "I'll be right in."

I put the car in park and cut the engine. Through the windshield, I watched as Nina stiff-armed the diner's swinging door and blew past a kitschy-looking older

woman at the front — the hostess, presumably. I tracked
Nina for a moment, past the pastry display and a couple of
empty booths, before a strange noise brought my attention
back inside the car. Nina's phone was vibrating in the cup
holder, jangling some coins beneath it. A familiar icon and
color scheme flashed on the screen.

A Happiness Engine notification.

It could have been a prompt for feedback or an
update on her levels. I didn't check but pocketed the phone
and stepped out of the car.

Outside, it felt nice to stretch my legs, to remind
my limbs that they had comrades that could all work together. A long car ride will stiffen your muscles, for sure,
but it can also cage your mind. The open road, the chas-
ing down of a destination, never seemed to give me the
space it promised. Now I felt free. Off the road, off the grid,
skewing from my usual pattern. Staring ahead into a life
that I knew would switch scenes and emotional filters like
a manic kaleidoscope.

I reached the swinging door and pushed through
into a shallow entryway. A gumball machine and a gallery
wall of old photos confirmed the roadside authenticity of
the place. And the hostess, with her big hair and faded
pink t-shirt and multiple butterfly brooches, proved as bri-
colage and as friendly as she looked from afar. "Welcome,
honey," she said. "Just you today?"

She didn't mean anything by it, but it shook me.
Because I knew there was an alternate version of this story,

encoded in an email just a few months back, where I show up to this place alone.

"No, we're together," I said, motioning toward the back.

The hostess turned to see Nina advancing over the checkerboard floor, coming back from the restroom toward the front of the house. Nina saw us watching and smiled, then stopped about midway, chose a seat at the counter, and waved me over.

24115290R00080

Made in the USA
San Bernardino, CA
03 February 2019